SERVANT OF THE UNDEAD

ISABELLE DRAKE

For more information contact:
Riverdale Avenue Books
5676 Riverdale Avenue
Riverdale, NY 10471

www.riverdaleavebooks.com

Design by www.formatting4U.com
Cover by Scott Carpenter

Digital ISBN: 978-1-62601-446-6

Print ISBN: 978-1-62601-447-3

First Edition May 2018

Dedication

For Loyalty:
Wherever you are hiding, I will find you

Chapter One
"Do it."

Hayden Thomas shifted on the wooden captain's chair, trying without success to ease the stiffness in his spine. Whoever selected the chairs for the Boston Public Library obviously never sat in them. The damn things had no armrests and were crammed so close together Bates Hall looked like a cafeteria. Except for the green desk lamps and rows of bookcases lining the wood paneled walls of the vast, deserted room. Hayden leaned back, placing his palms on the small of his back as he stretched.

Fine, it did look like a library. And it was everything the city claimed it to be, historical, well cared for, and a fucking architectural gem. He just didn't want to be there, digging through old books sane people shouldn't care about. As if on cue his phone flashed. He picked it up and read the message. *That article will be done tonight. Right? You'll have something fresh. Right?*

As if he had a choice. Tuesday by midnight, his weekly deadline.

Hayden tapped in his reply, *yes and yes*, then shoved the phone in his pocket. He wasn't going to look at it again until he had what he needed. Something *fresh*. What the hell did that mean anyway? A paycheck.

Control over his future. Little things like that. So he'd come to the library, to look through actual books. He'd scanned through several about werewolves, then set aside the ones on vampires when he found the ones he needed.

Coming to the library had been a good idea. Not only had he found *fresher* content than the guys only using the internet, but he'd also made a video clip of the interior with his webcam. He might be able to use that on the paper's website as part of the series. A scholarly approach to give the piece an air of authority. Bob would love the irony of that.

"Lights in this section getting turned off early. 'Bout 20 minutes."

The security guard had come up behind Hayden and was standing in the aisle between the rows of gleaming wood tables. He motioned toward the expansive windows that started at the top of the bookshelves and reached up about 15 feet to the domed ceiling. "Snowmaggeddon, man. Everybody's leaving. You should too."

Outside, snow whipped against the glass, so fierce and bright that even though the sun had gone down an hour ago, the white blast was still visible. The bloated flakes brushed against the glass, spun in circles, creating a delicate, menacing spiral. Shit. A storm. As if he didn't have enough to deal with. He'd promised Rachelle, a girl he'd started seeing, that he'd be done with the article that night so they could "do something fun, something crazy" tomorrow. Hayden eyed the stack of books surrounding his laptop.

"Do you have a photocopy machine?" he asked, scanning the area behind the guy.

"Yeah." The guard looked at the piles of books,

his mouth twisting into a frown as his gaze skimmed over the titles. "Where'd you find those?"

"In the scary monster section, under Z for zombies."

"Seriously, dude. I need to learn how to protect myself." The man whipped a folded newspaper out of his back pocket and brandished it, showing the headline. "It's all in here— *Zombies Flooding Beantown Streets, Hungry for Human Flesh.*" Hayden didn't need to see it in print because he'd come up with it when Bob insisted they write some pieces connected to the comic convention beginning that upcoming weekend.

"You believe what you read in *The Boston Weekly*?"

"They wouldn't print it if it wasn't true." The man folded the paper and tucked it back into his pocket. "Or could be true."

No wonder Bob Keeler had enough money to live in Chestnut Hill.

"The copier?"

The man pointed to a hall tucked between two bookcases. "It's down there. But like I said, you better get going." He stepped away, then turned back, his gaze hopping from one book to the next before finally landing on Hayden's face. "Snowmaggeddon. Zombies. Be careful. Article says to avoid isolated places and stay with others."

"I get it," Hayden assured him, using his firmest professor voice, the one he'd perfected while being a grad assistant at Boston College.

The guy gave Hayden the once over, doubt lining his face as he turned, the folded paper waving at Hayden as he marched off.

That teacher voice was handy, but according to Rachelle, he used it—and the attitude that came with

3

it—too much. She complained about his work ethic and said they needed to have more 'epic fun.' How was he supposed to have any kind of fun when he had years of student loan payments coming his way and only a one page CV to deal with them?

He swung out of the chair, grabbed the three books he hadn't gotten to yet, and headed for the hall. The photocopier, positioned under a rectangular window, hummed in the dimly lit space. He lifted the lid, set the book on the glass surface and started flipping through, scanning for the chapter he needed for his research. *Research*. Right. There was a euphemism. He jerked through the pages, black-eyed stares and ragged clothes flashed past. Good God. Zombies. Why did people waste their time with this sort of thing?

But Bob Keeler was convinced that because Rodney McKinnon, star of *Zombie Rites*, was coming to the comic convention, that if the paper featured anything having to do with zombies, especially something *fresh*, that he'd sell thousands of copies. The man was crazy. Sure, Boston was going to be overrun with comic book freaks. But those people were educated, right? They didn't believe zombies were real. So why would they want to read about them?

Hayden flipped to a chapter where the zombies looked like regular, living, people. No rotting flesh, no odd jerky movements. His skin prickled. *What if you couldn't tell a zombie from a normal human?* He paused at a drawing made by an eyewitness, a so-called zombie tracker. Apparently, the witness spent an entire summer stalking a tribe believed to take part in hazing rituals that included a lot of sex. The drawing showed two men, bare-chested and wearing chaps. One had a rope tied around his waist leaning against a tree while the other man tied the opposite end of rope to the trunk, tying him up like a dog so he wouldn't get away. Hayden lifted the book closer. They weren't wearing anything under the chaps. And the tied-up guy had a huge boner.

He turned the page. More drawings. The guy tied to the tree held the ass of a woman and was pounding that boner into her. Apparently, the witness had in mind to document the entire ritual. There were five more drawings, each one showing the man fucking a different woman while others watched. And all the women looked very satisfied. And willing.

Hayden's cock stiffened.

Okay, so they're people into group sex, but where was the proof they were zombies? Proof that zombies are real. He snickered. *That* would be fresh, so *that's* what he needed. What he didn't need was the distraction of a rock-hard dick. He reached down and shifted the zipper on his khakis.

The last page in the section outlined the zombie tracker's theory of that particular tribe's sexuality. Those zombies could remain "alive" by either eating human flesh or through frequent sex. The sex method worked because the live human passed out afterward, giving the zombie an opportunity to escape. Sometimes humans were taken as sexual servants, kept like pets and used for sustenance. The sexual hazing rituals were designed to encourage survival skills and teach tools to acquire and use humans.

Overhead, a window squeaked open. Gusts of snow flew in. Fingers scratched at the sill, clawing at the wood trim. A full hand appeared, covered with a black fingerless glove. The other hand appeared. Then a forearm, wrapped in red wool, an elbow, bare skin peaking out between the strips of red. A mass of tangled hair, a mix of brown and red, popped through the opening. One of the hands reached over, swiping the hair away. Two brown eyes, rimmed with smudgy make-up peered down.

"Give me a hand?" she said, her voice rough, probably from climbing up the side of the building. One of her hands started to slide, and she used her elbow to brace herself in the frame. "Please?" Snow and wind blew in, slickening the sill and her elbow started to slide. "Hurry."

Hayden glanced down the hall, but he was surrounded by dim silence. That security guard was probably combing the stacks, looking for anyone else desperate enough to be at the library in the middle of a snowstorm. Or, more likely, trying to find the scary monster section. The coast was clear, so he pulled a chair over and stepped on to the seat.

He reached up. "Give me your hand."

Clouds of snow blew in, blinding Hayden, but he reached up, grabbing for the girl. His hands connected with something wet and cold, an arm maybe, and he curled his fingers around icy flesh.

"I think I have you," he said, trying to look up but getting a face full of snow.

"Pull me in."

Hayden yanked until he heard a yelp.

"Okay, stop. I can climb down from here."

"You sure?" he asked, still holding on.

"Yes. Get out of the way."

6

Hayden squared himself. "I'm not sure I care for your tone."

The girl's voice came again, the hesitation completely gone. "Get out of the way or I'm going to land on you."

"Suit yourself," Hayden said, stepping off the chair.

Between gusts of wind and snow, a body appeared. Somehow she'd managed to turn herself around in the window, spinning so her legs, covered in tattered black fishnets, came down first. Booted feet landed on top of the copier. A tiny, midnight blue skirt barely covered her ass. Her torso was wrapped in some kind of red sweater that left parts of her skin exposed. Once she was fully out of the window and standing on the copier, she reached up on tiptoe, closed the window and turned around.

Hayden looked up her skirt and caught a glimpse of skin. The fishnets were real stockings. That meant her thighs were bare. What if she wasn't wearing panties? Her pussy would be—

"Do you always have such an attitude when someone asks for help?" She put her hands on her hips, her long fingers flashing white in the fingerless gloves, and looked down at him. Her arched back made her breasts look huge.

Instead of waiting for an answer, she dropped down to sit on the copier, then hopped down to the floor. Correction. Her breasts *were* huge. Tumblr worthy, for sure.

Shit. His hard dick had conjured her up.

She lifted her hands to smack snow from her hair, her breasts shaking from the movement. Maybe the sweater would give way on its own? A scent drifted

7

through the air and settled in the back of his mouth, on his teeth—bitter, like the smell of blood.

"You're not very friendly. Is there anyone else here?" she asked, running her hands across her arms and legs, spreading snow onto the floor and flicking some on to him.

Obviously he hadn't conjured her up, because if he had she wouldn't be looking for anyone else besides him, and she sure as hell wouldn't be using that tone. And that smell—he wouldn't have added that, couldn't have imagined a scent so insidious, one that filled his mouth, making him salivate and gage at the same time.

"It's a bit snowy out there." He swallowed, clearing his throat. "I think the flurries might be keeping people at home." If she noticed his sarcasm, she didn't respond. She didn't seem to notice his rude staring, either, so he kept on. If she wasn't going to bother being polite he wasn't either.

Her nipples were peaked tight, rubbing against the red fabric. The scent faded. Either that or he stopped caring. "Aren't you cold?" he asked, staring at the red material wrapped around her torso. It wasn't really a sweater; it looked more like a strip of fabric spun around her like a giant ace bandage.

She finally got the last of the snow off, but her clothes were soaked and clinging. Even so, she wasn't shivering. Didn't even look cold. Or concerned about the oddness of climbing in through a library window in the middle of a storm. Hayden backed up and she came closer, then brushed past him and marched halfway down the hall, her skirt brushing against her thighs. Hayden started wondering about panties again.

She definitely seemed like the kind of girl who would go without. When she reached the end of the hall, she looked from side to side, then strutted back, coming straight for him.

"You're right about the storm, and it's empty on the streets, too. That's why I came in here," she said, her voice switching to an awkward sweetness when she continued. "You are the only person around."

"There's a security guard."

Her lip curled. "Doesn't sound like a good idea. Not the kind of man I'm looking for." She moved forward, swaying so that the hem of her skirt came up, showing the tops of her stockings.

Obviously, this girl was trouble with a capital T, and Hayden had spent his whole life avoiding trouble, playing it safe and getting things done. He backed up, reaching for the stack of books he'd left on top of the copier. Never mind the copies. He tucked the books under his arm and marched back the way he'd come. He didn't even take one last look at her gorgeous round breasts, pouty lips, or fishnet-covered legs. No need, really. He wouldn't be forgetting any of the details any time soon.

"Wait!" she called after him, and he heard the thud of her boots as she took off.

The even rhythm followed him all the way to the table where he'd left his things. He set the books down and started putting his papers into folders. She came up behind him and wrapped her arms around his waist.

"Um, hi?" she said, her smudgy eyes taking on a desperate sheen. "My name's Mattie, by the way."

Hayden reached over, trying to X out of the update email he'd been writing to Bob Keeler so he could shut down his computer. Her hands slid down from his waist, over his ass, and around thighs, the light pressure easily heating him up even through the thick material of his pants. Trying to ignore her and his lust, he jabbed at the keyboard, hitting whatever he could reach. He had to get the hell out of there before he started acting on the fantasies flickering in the back of his mind. This girl was going to get him into trouble, somehow. He just knew it. "I really have to get going."

"But, you—I—" Mattie rolled herself around him, hopped onto the table, and wrapped her legs around him. She reached behind to brace herself with her hands but slipped back when her palm landed on one of the books. She looked back, stayed still for a few seconds, slid the books around, running her hands over the titles. "You're reading about zombies?"

Hayden cleared his throat. "It's research."

"What did you find out?" she asked, flipping open the book with the pictures.

He reached around and pushed the book closed. "Nothing."

She opened another, thumbed through the pages. "What were you looking for?"

"Anything. Nothing. Whatever I can find."

She spun around and shimmied, her breasts bouncing. "I can help. What do you need?"

"Thanks, but I don't think you can help. Unless you have proof that zombies are real. Like some pictures, you know. They're combing the streets, looking for flesh. Haven't you heard?"

She grinned up at him, her eyes shining with unmistakable lust. Was it for the zombies or him? "Sounds scary," she said, lifting her eyebrows.

"Scary is right. If I don't get something *fresh about zombies* my editor probably won't give me any more special assignments."

She didn't say anything, just sat there rocking her shoulders, staring at him with her smudgy eyes, licking her pouty lips and looking exactly like a Barbie doll gone bad.

Why was he talking with her anyway?

Hayden tried to free himself from her thighs, but she was stronger than she looked. A lot stronger. He reached down to pry her legs off, but the rows of table lights went off, and he was blinded. His eyes began to adjust, making use of the light from the street lamps coming through the windows. It was flickering from the snow, so it was still difficult to see clearly. He fought her legs again, pulling in a deep breath as he did. That scent settled across his tongue, spread to his teeth, making his mouth open.

Hayden gave up trying to break free from her legs and reached for her chin, tipping her face up to try and reason with her. "I think this section is closing, so—" When their gaze connected, his words fell away. Her eyes flickered in the darkness, glowing green.

She blinked, but the gleam came back as soon as her gaze found his again. It wasn't the snow casting the light in her eyes. It was something inside her. Something that explained why she was climbing around in the night, not wearing a coat, not cold. Hayden slid his palm across her neck to settle on her throat. There had to be a pulse.

Of course.

He was being totally ridiculous.

Just to be sure, he slid his hand down lower,

11

stopping over her heart. The thick straps were in the way, so he tucked his fingers under them, stopping when he felt the swell of her breast. Before he could feel her heartbeat, she laid her hand across his and guided it lower, brushing his palm across her nipple. The peak tightened and she sighed softly, the sound a cross between a moan and whimper.

Hayden tried to move his hand lower, to feel the weight of her breast in his palm, but the straps were too tight, and his hand wouldn't move. A thread of panic ignited his nerves, and he tugged. She moaned again, reached up to pull the straps from her other breast and pinch her own nipple, wiggling with satisfaction. His cock responded, the sudden flow of blood making him impossibly hard.

She dropped her hand and reached for his belt, her fingers working quickly to undo the buckle, the snap, and zipper. His cock jutted straight out, ready to thrust into her pussy despite the confusion and anxiety swirling through him. He tugged at his hand again, and it finally came free. But he was still held captive by her legs. With strong, sharp motions, she yanked him closer, tightening the grip around his waist as she lifted her skirt.

The black fishnet stockings ended near the juncture of her thighs, just as he'd imagined and she was, in fact, without panties.

The dark wood of the table contrasted with her light skin, and the smooth lips of her pussy were slick and ready. The possibility of trouble was still there, but this other possibility—doing something crazy—was the one he was paying attention to. His dick was so hard he could drive into her with one thrust, he was sure of it.

12

Hayden grabbed her thighs, spread her legs and swung her forward, angling her so her hot sheath opened completely. He inched closer, so the tip of his penis touched her wet skin.

"Do it," she whispered. "Fuck me."

He drove in, filling her just like he knew he would, and groaned. The tight walls of her core gripped him, squeezing his shaft, making it harder, bigger. She grabbed his shoulders and rocked against him, gliding her pussy up and down his cock, taking control.

Hayden bent lower, reaching for her free breast with his tongue, wanting to feel it inside his mouth. He found the nipple, but the mound was too full and her motions too frenzied, so he had to settle for licking the tip.

She grunted in response, her hips jerking as she rocked against him, taking his entire shaft inside her and pushing against his balls with each forward swing. His sac heated, his whole body tingled with fire. His cock was deep inside her, wrapped in her cunt, but the connection wasn't enough. He lifted his mouth from her breast, seeking her lips. Just as he brushed his mouth against hers, she stiffened and groaned.

He pressed his mouth against her cool, wet lips. She sucked in a breath of sharp surprise, tried to kiss him back, but the spirals of release took possession of her body. She thrashed against him, forcing his hard cock deep inside her as her breathing turned into a series of short pants. Hayden pressed a kiss across her open lips, then let himself go, falling into his own explosive bliss. Tight piercing pleasure coiled through him as his own orgasm hit, hard and fast.

13

They clung to each other, their bodies recovering from the shared explosion.

"Thanks," she said, after a pause, looking up at him from under her tangled locks. "I really needed that." She started putting her clothes back together, adjusting the straps to cover her breasts.

Hayden laughed lightly as he gently pulled up his briefs and pants, trying not to brush against his cock, which was still slightly erect. "You don't need to say thanks. I wanted it."

"Hey! Anyone in here?"

Shit. The security guard. Still zipping his pants, Hayden called out *hello* as he jogged through the darkness.

"You're still in here, in the dark?" the guard looked past Hayden's shoulder. "Everything okay?"

Hayden stepped closer, blocking his view. "I'm fine, just packing up, about to head home."

The guard ran his flashlight beam around the room, but the small ray didn't do much to light up the huge space. "Snow's not letting up, just so you know."

Trying to look casual, not like a guy who'd just had frantic sex, Hayden shoved his hands in his pockets and slouched his shoulders. "Good to know."

"Stay safe, man."

"Right. Thanks." Hayden spun around and headed back. She was gone. Probably climbed back out the window. Or climbed out of his freshly ignited imagination.

Hayden tapped his computer. The message to Bob Keeler popped up. He added a quick note about writing something about hot zombie sex rituals, attached the video of the library, and hit send. With a heavy thump, he dropped into the stiff chair and

14

reached for the files. In a minute, he'd get everything pulled together and get going. That fresh stuff wasn't going to appear out of nowhere.

* * *

The vibrating of his phone woke Hayden, and still half-asleep, he dug it out of his pocket and answered, his eyes still closed.

"Hayden. You are a genius."

Struggling against a serious kink in his back, Hayden worked his way into a sitting position. "Thanks, Bob," he said, even though he had no idea what the man was all worked up about.

"The film tie-in idea is awesome. Perfect. That attachment, good grief. Why didn't you tell me you were a Photoshop wiz?"

Starting to actually wake up, Hayden looked around. The library? He'd fallen asleep at the table when he was supposed to be reading those damn zombie books. Shit. Hazy images of a wet girl with tangled hair and torn tights flashed in his mind. A smell. Mind-blowing sex. Holy shit. What a dream.

"Good thing Rachelle is the wild type. Most girls wouldn't want pictures of their guy screwing some other girl, even a zombie, posted all over the net."

Hayden snapped awake. "Posted?"

"Absolutely." Bob chuckled, then lowered his voice. "That sex video was hot, Hayden, but a bit over the top. Even for us. So Chuck cut it into stills, and our hit counter is already popping."

Sex video?

"Popping?" Hayden said, starting to sweat. He

15

grabbed his laptop and typed in the newspaper's link. The home page was filled with a woman's dark silhouette, the pale skin of one of her big breasts peeking between the red wraps, the other was blacked out with a solid square. Her wet, matted hair was tangled around her shoulders, her eyes were unmistakably glowing green, and the man positioned between her legs was obviously him.

A neon blue banner ran through the middle of the page: *Zombie sex ritual uncovered! Everyday men seduced by the undead!*

"A bonus check is already in your mail box, Hayden. You really came through for me, kid. Thanks."

"Sure thing." Hayden clicked off, but didn't set his phone down. Even though they'd only been together a short while, Rachelle should hear about the pictures from him.

He hit her number and settled back to wait, but she answered right away.

"What the hell, Hayden?"

"You already know, huh," he replied, hitting the link to move away from the home page.

"Yes. And I am pissed."

The next page was another shot of him and the girl, her white fingers curled over her own breast while his hand was obviously trapped in the red straps. "How did you find out?"

"Bob."

"Bob?" *Thanks Bob, for adding to my list of failed relationships.*

"Yeah, he wanted to make sure it was okay with me before he put the pictures up."

Hayden scrolled down, the next picture showed Mattie's thigh, half-covered by the tattered fishnets, tightly wrapped around his hips. The tiny skirt covered up his cock, thrusting in and out of her. "And it's okay with you?" he said, his voice nearly squeaking.

"Yes. But I'm still pissed."

He scrolled down again. It was shot of Mattie's face, her smudgy, glowing eyes staring straight at the screen. A chill ran down his spine. Straight to his dick, which was getting hard again. "It's just that, I—"

"I've been after you to do something crazy and you had this kinky side all along. I'm pissed you kept it a secret." She sighed, impatient and annoyed. "Why Hayden? Don't you get that I want you for who you are, not because I'm waiting around for you to make stacks of money."

Hayden X'ed out of the website. "Oh."

"I'm coming over to your apartment, tonight. I'll be wearing—oh no, I'm not telling. It's going to be a surprise. A hot, sexy surprise. And you better be ready to fuck me senseless. That's the only way I'm going to forgive you for keeping secrets."

Another turn in a night that didn't make sense. But Hayden was done being cautious and careful. He scrambled to his feet and adjusted his khakis, but there was no hiding his solid erection. He stashed his laptop into his backpack and started walking, leaving the zombie books on the table.

"Don't make me wait," she snapped, then clicked off.

Hayden charged into the snowy night and didn't look back.

Chapter Two
"Don't make me wait."

Hayden burst out of the library and charged face-first into the storm. A nasty blast of wind whipped past, filling his nose with giant flakes and blinding him. He slipped on his gloves to wipe his eyes, then hitched up his backpack and tightened the front strap. After wrapping his itchy black wool scarf tightly around his neck, Hayden took the first careful step. Thick, wet snow sagged until his boot finally hit the concrete. Three slow, leaping strides later, he reached the landing of the low steps that led to Dartmouth Street, snow-covered and silent. Not a single living person was out on the streets.

Once he got back to his borrowed apartment, he planned to stay put and wait the storm out too. Apparently, he was going to be at Rachelle's mercy the whole time. At first he'd been anxious about hooking up with a neighbor, but now he was really beginning to see the advantage to having her in the brownstone right next door. A hot flush washed over him, chasing away a sliver of the monstrous chill following him down the hushed street. He kept moving, closer to Rachelle and farther away from that unbelievable scene. Sex, video, and a lie more believable than the truth.

The drifts of dense, untouched snow made walking difficult, and the cold air was beginning to pierce his lungs, making each breath a whisper of pain, but he moved on, slowly, steadily—determined and clinging to Rachelle's demand.

Be ready to fuck me senseless.

He was ready. He just had to get there first.

An unnatural mixture of light came from buildings, the moon and the eerie brightness of the unrelenting storm. The historic Old South Church was behind him on his right, stoic and solid. The garish light of a 7-Eleven blinked up ahead on the left, red, green and promising 24-hour access to Slurpees, cigarettes and bullshit junk food. Even in the blizzard the contrast was jarring.

On the backside of the Old South Church, an open window smacked against the stone exterior of the wide building. Weak light shone from within. Wind howled up Dartmouth Street, cold, biting bursts of snow-filled air, bitter like the ice of the Charles River about ten blocks away. The window snapped shut with a crack, then burst open again. Inside the church, the light faded.

Hayden winced, forcing his gaze away from the church and his legs farther into Boston's Back Bay. Of course there was nothing to see in that window—no girl with dark eyes, smudged with black eyeliner, and D-size breasts wrapped in strips of red wool. Crazy thing was, if he told someone he'd done some random girl at the library—right there on one of the sturdy oak tables, they'd probably be jealous. Or at least smack him a high five. Hell, the whole thing fit together like a fantasy from an old sci-fi pulp paperback. But now that he was away from the girl, he felt anything but fantastic. Whatever sexual spell she'd cast over him had faded, and he was reconsidering his state of mind.

And, he realized, reconsidering the girl.

Her scent.

Her physical strength.

Her power over him.

Unable to stop himself, he glanced back, searching through the whipping snow, scanning the wall of the church, tracing the points of the Gothic arches until he spotted the window. It was still open, still swinging slightly, and still empty.

Thank God.

Clutching the straps of his backpack, he trudged on, concentrating on maintaining a smooth, steady rhythm. The few blocks to Commonwealth Avenue went quickly enough, and once he spotted the rows of lighted trees lining the boulevard, the tension in his spine eased, and the lingering anxiety lifted. Even muted by the heavy snow, the tiny white holiday lights brightened the fierceness of the weather, making it almost postcard pretty, instead of what it actually was—a monster of a storm that had choked the life out of the entire city.

Hayden lifted his scarf to cover his mouth and pull in a warm breath. The air filled his chilled lungs. *Relax.* He had a hot girl waiting for him and, thanks to an accidental video, a bonus check on the way. Life— or at least that night—was damn near perfect.

That was his last thought before spotting a familiar pair of heavy black boots peeking out from beside the snow-heaped bushes lining the front of his brownstone. He didn't need to run his gaze up the long, lean legs covered in tattered fishnets and see that nearly pointless miniskirt to know it was her sitting on the steps.

The solid, booted feet swung in, disappearing. The air in Hayden's lungs went cold and came out in a raw rush. Wind howled behind him, pushing him forward, propelling him. Same as when they'd been together in the library, her face was plain, her gaze scanning the area around them in quick sharp sweeps. But this time she wasn't looking for just anyone. She was waiting for him. And all traces of sweetness were gone.

"You thinking about paying those bills?" she asked, pointing to his backpack as she swung forward, her boots sliding easily into the deep drifts beside the bush. "It's going to suck if they shut off your wireless."

Hayden shoved his scarf below his chin. "It's rude to go through other people's shit."

She set her hands on her hips and arched her back, forcing her incredible breasts into his line of vision. "How else was I going to figure out where to find you?"

"Why did you need to find me at all?" he asked, trying to circle her, to get away from her and the wrongness that was now seeping into the night. Two steps and already he felt the sensation of the smell settling deep in his mouth, seeping across his molars. His mouth opened.

She watched his lips part as she moved with him, gliding, matching his movement as though she anticipated each step.

"Is it about the pictures? The ones posted on the *Weekly*'s site?" he asked.

She kept moving with him, her brown eyes taking on the green sheen he'd thought he'd imagined in the library. "Yeah, it was the pictures," she murmured, "but not how you think." She tucked her fingers under of the strips of wet wool circling her torso and tugged. Bare white skin peeked between the wraps as she shimmied to adjust them. Not that her changes did any good. The full curves of her breasts and the tight peaks of her nipples were still totally obvious. Then again, maybe that was her point.

Hayden ground his teeth, trying to crush the sensation in his jaw, but couldn't pull his gaze away from her glistening, exposed body. Tiny icicles clung to the tangles of her hair and flakes of snow dotted her thighs, bare above the edge of the tights. He cleared his throat, trying to keep his mind from acknowledging the blood flowing to his cock. "The guy I work for thinks they're a great tie-in to the zombie stuff—my piece, the comic convention and the opening of *Zombie Rites*. And all that stuff about zombies—"

"Roaming the streets?" she cut in, grinning as she dropped her hand to smack snow off her limp skirt. Once she got the clumps off, she ran her fingers across the hem, inching it up her bare thighs.

Holy fuck, he was starting to remember what it felt like to be inside her. Driving into her tight core, pounding until he couldn't think straight.

Hayden glanced at the apartment. Rachelle was not peering out the window, watching for him. Thank God. He shifted back. Most girls would probably get pretty pissed at a guy who took a video of himself grinding his dick into her, but this girl seemed anything but pissed. Hayden found himself watching the flicker of her stubby black fingernails as she inched up the hem of her skirt. He knew she wasn't wearing panties. Five inches was all it would take and her bare pussy—

He took a sharp step forward, ready to shove her out of the way if necessary. She grabbed his arm and jerked him close enough for her nipples to brush against him.

"My girlfriend is waiting for me," he said, pointing to the third story of the brownstone.

Mattie tossed back her mass of hair, exposing a small black device tucked into her ear. "I know. 'Don't make me wait.' Isn't that what she said?" A cruel smile tugged on the corner of her full mouth as she took in his expression. "You don't understand yet, do you? Let me explain. You belong to me now. Until I'm done with you, that is." She forced one of her legs between his thighs and lifted until her knee pressed into his solid cock. "I'm liking you more and more, so we may be together a while."

Hayden jerked his arms free and reached for her pale throat. The skin beneath his palms was wet, slick, smooth. And cold, lifeless.

"Go up there and fuck your *girlfriend*," she said, then shoved him away and moved toward the wall of the row house. She propped her booted foot on the cornerstone and lifted herself. She slithered up; her hands clutching the frost-covered bricks, then paused about ten feet from the ground. "And make it hot. Because I'll be watching." And with that, she crept up to the third-floor window and nestled under the eave.

23

* * *

Still feeling the soul-stealing gaze of Mattie's cold, hungry eyes, Hayden jogged up the snow-covered steps. After kicking the heavy, white heap away from the door, he pulled it open and stumbled inside. A gust of icy air and cloud of flakes followed him in, blasting his face and sending a sharp chill down his neck. Once the door was closed tight, he paused, looking through the beveled glass, searching through the blizzard-filled night. Of course she wasn't there where he could see her.

She was hovering above the window, waiting.

A new type of shiver worked its way down his spine. A fierce tremor that he didn't know but understood.

Do it.

Whatever she wanted, he would. If only to manage her until he could get control, decide what to do next. Hell, he needed more than control—he needed to find a way to get rid of her.

Breathing in a lungful of pure, warm air, he headed up the stairs, each step filling him deeper with a new dread—bringing Rachelle into whatever it was he had with Mattie. He would make it all right, manage the situation. Somehow. As long as Rachelle didn't come in contact with Mattie, he could keep her out of it. Whatever *it* was that he'd gotten himself into.

The landing of the third floor was smaller than the other two because there was only one apartment on that floor. Rachelle was waiting for him there, standing next to the open door with her back against the wall. She was wrapped in a long brown fur coat, the smug expression on her face confirming that she expected nothing less than a scorching-hot, mind-blowing fuck.

Tapping one bright-pink nail on the plush collar, she asked, "Remember this?" She smiled and swayed lightly as she held the coat tightly against herself.

Hayden let out a thick breath and eased his shoulders back. His book bag bumped his thigh. "Yep." He eyed the coat, a bundle of fur that probably cost a year's tuition. "You had it on the first night we met."

She nodded, stroking the fur with two fingers. "I still feel a bit bad for ditching that other guy."

Her words were a lie and they both knew it. Rachelle rarely felt bad about anything she did.

"He was in over his head," Hayden replied with a shrug, remembering the way the poor man kept glancing at the door every time Rachelle touched his arm. "He knew it, though," Hayden continued, but even as the words fell from his lips he was suddenly reconsidering the other man's response to Rachelle. Maybe the guy had been looking for a way out because he'd sensed Rachelle was the type of woman to pull a man down the wrong path.

Why hadn't Hayden considered that before?

"Stop looking like that," Rachelle said. "It's too late to worry about him now." She ran her fingertips down his damp sleeve. The collar of the heavy coat fell forward, revealing very expensive-looking, intricate black lace lingerie that shoved her breasts upward into his line of view. The gentle swells were impressive, but not in the dangerously sexy way Mattie's tits demanded attention.

A fat drop of melted snow ran down the side of

25

his face, trickling its way to his neck. Rachelle was right. It was too late. Too late for her. For him. He clenched his jaw, fighting a roll of anger.

Feeling the threat lingering outside, he grabbed both of Rachelle's wrists and lifted her arms above her head. He leaned into her and used his weight to press her to the wall. "I don't want to think about that night anymore."

Her bright-blue eyes gleamed. "Are you going to apologize for keeping secrets and not telling me you had such a naughty side?"

What kind of girl gets turned-on by her guy screwing around with another woman? Maybe he didn't know Rachelle as well as he thought. Maybe he didn't really know her at all.

Hayden ran his mouth down her throat then straightened, taking his time to gaze across the black lace covering her breasts. Still holding her to the wall, he angled back and checked out the matching garter belt and panties. Sheer stockings covered her legs. "I don't feel sorry," he said. It was mostly true.

She ran her tongue between her lips, then bit her lip. It was a coy move he'd seen before, but this time he understood it was anything but the shy response of an inexperienced girl.

"How *do* you feel?" she asked.

"Ready to fuck you senseless. As requested."

"What are you waiting for?"

Hayden released her arms then shoved her through the open door. He didn't wait for her to catch her balance. He pushed her again, shoving her through the living room, down the hall and onto his bed. She fell in a heap then rolled onto her back.

Still on his feet, he could stop now and risk not

giving the creature outside what she wanted. But even as he considered the possibility, he knew he wasn't going to stop. It was a wish, a pointless idea that he had any way to control the wild thing that had crawled into his life. Until he had a plan to get rid of her, she was going to take whatever she wanted from him and he was going to keep giving until she didn't want any more. His immediate concern—find a way to keep Rachelle as safe as possible. Right then, that meant fucking her.

Rachelle's heavy coat had come mostly off, and she was clinging to it as though it could somehow help her maintain her dignity. As though the coat could somehow hide the truth of who she really was, a girl about to be used by a boyfriend she didn't really know while a creature perched on the ledge outside watched.

Hayden set his book bag by his desk and started shrugging out of his coat. Once he had it off, he peeled away his scarf, gloves. Kicked off his boots. Then he tugged his sweater up and off.

Rachelle had rolled onto her side. Her bra twisted, and one of her nipples showed above the lace. When she started to gather the coat to toss it to the floor, he shook his head. "Leave it."

As she shoved the fur beneath her, he threw his shirt down, kicked off his pants.

Rachelle pulled her knees up, let her legs fall apart, and then closed her knees again. "I stayed around even though you kept fucking me vanilla-style because I *just knew* you had a dirty side."

Mattie's green gaze flashed in his mind, and he remembered the other girl lifting her miniskirt for him, right there in the middle of the library. The tight grip of her slick, wet channel and the way he pumped into

27

her right there on the library table.

"You don't know the half of it," he said, his gaze going to the window. The blizzard was still fierce, but thanks to the street lamps he could see into the swirls of snow. He crossed the room and peered out, looking right, then left, searching until he found her.

Still hunched under the eave, she crept forward, sneered, and then inched forward. Hayden breathed in through his nostrils and let the air out slowly through his mouth. Outside, the thing nodded, assuring him she was going to get what she wanted. Again, she crept closer, smiling in her unsmiling way, as she moved sure and steady like the storm.

Hayden moved away from the window, spinning on his heels so the window was at his back. He could block the creature from his sight, but not from his mind. She was already controlling him in ways he was only beginning to suspect. The image in his mind of what he wanted to do to the girl in his bed was just one of those ways.

Rachelle lay before him, opening and closing her legs, showing off the smooth skin of her inner thighs and the delicate lace covering her pussy. No matter that she was, in truth, a spoiled daddy's girl, she didn't deserve this. What he was doing was wrong and he knew it. Yet he wouldn't stop. Couldn't stop.

Maybe the effect the creature was having on him could actually be a good thing. Revealing it to Rachelle would show her she needed to leave him, and she would be free of the danger.

"Take off your stockings," he said, nodding to the black silk skimming her thighs and calves.

Rachelle was quick to do his bidding, unhooking

the garter tabs with an unsuspecting smile. She rolled the right stocking down, shook it with a flick of her wrist tossing it toward him. It landed near at the foot of the bed, a sheer snake stretched across the cream velvet cover. She took off the other in the same way, removed the belt, then dropped back onto her elbows.

Hayden had taken off the rest of his clothes and stood naked, his body tense, his soul clouded. He picked up a stocking, slid it across his palm. "You sure you're ready for this?" he asked, pulling it taut with his fists.

"Yes Sir."

"Let's start with a couple rules." He set the stocking back down and took a step forward, conscious of his hard dick jutting out in front of him. "I have two."

"Not three?" She cocked her head and looked sideways at him. "Don't rules always come in threes?"

"Not from me. I have two." Hayden came around to the side of the bed. "Do you agree?"

"Aren't you going to tell me what they are?"

"Nope." He thrust his hips forward, and the tip of his shaft pressed against her lifted leg. "You agree to follow the rules, then I tell them to you, then we go ahead."

She pouted, her pink lips forming a soft rounded hole he thought about shoving his cock into. "And if I don't?" she asked. Already he knew she would obey. It was obvious in the quick rise of her chest and the dark, lust-filled gaze of her eyes. But she had no way of knowing he intended to push her far past her limits.

Hayden rocked his hips again, quicker than the first time so she couldn't miss the incredible stiffness.

"You're going to agree to whatever I say. We both know it. But I want to hear you say it."

"I'll follow your rules," she said.

Hayden snatched up his scarf then circled the bed so that the view from the window was clear. "Rule one—do whatever I say."

Rachelle stretched out, spreading her arms across the coat beneath her as she tilted her head back and looked up at him from half-closed eyes. "I'll do whatever you say."

"Sit up and take off the bra."

She did.

"Give me your hands."

She offered him her hands, and he wrapped the scarf around her wrists, looping it between her hands so that when he tied the ends to the bedpost it would be harder for her to get free. Once her arms were securely tied above her head, he went back to the foot of the bed to retrieve one of the stockings.

"What are you going to do with that?" she asked, her voice a curious purr.

"Rule number two." He tugged on the stocking. "Don't speak unless I ask you to."

She chuckled. "Are you serious?"

He intentionally ignored her question as he wrapped the stocking around the base of his stiff cock then tugged. The pressure increased, and he moaned with the need for release. With each thump of his heart, the hot blood flowed in his veins, the pressure building, blocking out everything else in his mind. He lowered his other hand and caressed his shaft. The skin under his fingers was on fire. Even the lightest touch made his nerve endings skitter. The pleasure was so intense it bordered on pain, and he continued to stroke himself, feeling the last shreds of his human control slipping away.

Rachelle sucked in a sharp breath. Her shock motivated him to show her more. He wrapped the other end of the stocking around his tip. Once it was secure, he tugged lightly. The stab of pressure took his breath away, and for a split second he was lost, a captive of himself. He tugged again, almost hoping he would pass out from the force of the sensation. But the pain only served to heighten his awareness of Mattie's stare through the window, reaching him, touching him, even though she was yards away.

Finally, he loosened his grip, dropped his hands. His cock was impossibly stiff and tight, aching with need. "Do I look serious?" he asked, shocked at the roughness in his voice.

Rachelle's mouth opened, but just as quickly she snapped it shut and nodded.

Hayden grabbed the second stocking, moved back to the side of the bed, then wrapped it under her breasts. He secured it tightly, feeling the solid bones of her ribcage give slightly as he tugged. Her tits lifted and her nipples tightened. He licked the peaks. She arched her back and shoved more of her tender flesh between his teeth. Once he was sure her nipples were moist and hard, he took the other stocking and wrapped it above her breasts, again tightening the silk and applying gentle but firm pressure on her well-rounded mounds. There was enough length remaining from each stocking to secure them together in the center of the front. He wrapped the ends around a couple times. The final knot applied enough pressure to separate her breasts and create a pulling-pushing effect.

Her nipples were pointed and hard, her flesh firm and motionless. He reached forward and tapped each tight peak with his finger. "Do you like it?"

She nodded.

"You can speak when I ask you to," he said.

"I like it. Very much."

He reached between her legs, stroked her soft pussy through the black lace.

"See if you can get your panties off."

In response, she tugged on her arms, silently asking him to untie her. He shook his head. "Without your hands. If you want them off badly enough, you'll find a way."

She squirmed and the waistband twisted, exposing a tiny bit more of her smooth skin. She wiggled more, lowering the panties over her hipbones just an inch. After several sideways attempts to lower them more, she lifted her hips and scooted down as far as her tied arms would allow. Then she crept up, using the curve of her ass to force the sheer fabric lower. Each time she lifted her body, her back arched, forcing her breasts up, closer to his face.

Hayden gripped his shaft and stroked. The tight, warm skin felt good in his hand. Firm and alive. Very, very alive.

Still lifting and lowering, Rachelle started twisting her legs, bringing her knees together as she writhed on the bed. Most of her ass was exposed and the sloping curve of her pelvic bone and the light patch of hair were beginning to appear above the band of the panties.

Hayden continued stroking his cock, watching Rachelle struggle with her task. Her head was thrown

32

back, her lips open and moist, and the scent of her arousal filled his nostrils. As he stared, he was aware of the darkness swirling in his soul.

"I'm glad you're enjoying the challenge," he said, admiring her long, fluid motions.

She turned her head and their gazes connected for only a heartbeat before hers dropped to his hands. Hayden let go of his cock, took the panties in both hands, and yanked. She shifted, bringing her legs up so the scrap of fabric slid to her calves and then over her feet. He shoved her legs apart, then climbed between her knees.

Chapter Three
"I'll be watching."

A gust of wind howled past the window, rattling the pane. Hayden looked. Outside, in the night, gusts of white flakes circled and spun. He shifted, twisting to see farther. Even though he couldn't see her, not even the white flash of her cold fingers, he knew she was there. He knew because he felt her inside him.

Hayden turned back to the bed. The bursts of snow were so dense that the light from the street reflected off the flakes, casting shadows across Rachelle's body. The slick lips of her pussy glimmered in the pale sheen. He caressed her stomach, then put one palm on each thigh and made circles with his thumbs. It was a small touch, but she responded, dropping her knees lower. She wanted to say something, the question lingered in her gaze, but she didn't speak.

"Good girl," he said. "I'm glad you're following the rules."

The curve of her mouth softened and her lips parted as she lifted her head to look at his rock-hard cock.

Hayden thrust his hips forward and let the tip of his dick brush across her wet pussy. "I know what you need, but you're only going to get it when I'm ready to

34

give it to you." He rocked again, hard enough so his cock pushed between her slick lips. She squirmed and tugged on the ties holding her arms. "And you have to earn it."

He tilted his head toward the end of the bed. "Straighten yourself out." She followed his request instantly, sliding herself as best she could so that her body was long and flat. Once she was as straight as she could get, Hayden swung around so that he was facing the window and his back was to the headboard. He rose up and scooted back. As he worked himself over Rachelle's bound breasts, his cock brushed against one of her tight mounds. His balls rubbed across the stockings. Inch by inch he worked his way back. Once his ball sac was just above Rachelle's open mouth, he settled himself.

He stiffened, pausing to feel the caress of her breath across his tight skin. Each whisper of air came faster and harder than the one before. Hayden spread his arms as wide as he could and took hold of the headboard. He wanted to look at the ceiling, to avoid the call of the thing in the snow, but he couldn't.

This time when he looked outside, she was there, staring back at him through the single pane of glass. The weight of her gaze pressed across his entire body. His muscles tensed. He gripped the wood tighter, feeling the muscles in his arms and shoulders flex. The tension worked its way lower, each inch of his body turning hot and hard beneath the thick weight of her gaze.

She wanted a show.

"Lick me," he said to Rachelle. There was huskiness in his voice that not even he recognized.

35

She started to take his balls into her mouth. He lifted up. "No. Lick me."

He lowered. She complied, stretching her tongue up as far as it would go.

Hayden kept his gaze forward, refusing to admit to himself that he was afraid.

Beneath him, Rachelle continued licking his balls, her tongue working across his skin with steady and firm strokes. "That's right. Just like that."

Outside, Mattie moved closer to the glass, her face near enough that Hayden could see more than the cold hunger in her eyes. He saw things he never expected. Longing. Vulnerability.

While Rachelle continued licking all she could reach, Hayden's gaze stayed connected with the thing on the ledge. Mattie lifted her hand and laid her palm across the glass. She leaned forward, almost pressing her nose to the pane. A shiver of pity flashed through Hayden.

Beneath him, Rachelle moaned, and Hayden pulled his gaze away from the creature outside to the woman below. To make Rachelle safe, he had to push harder to get her to see, to feel, the threat of danger.

"That's enough licking," he said.

She stopped the motion of her mouth, but her body shifted, the strain of lust pulling her body taut. Ready.

Hayden avoided looking outside by turning his gaze to the ceiling. A lattice pattern made by the shadows of the street lamps glided across the surface, hanging above the bed like a cage.

"Take my whole cock in your mouth and suck until I come."

Immediately, she opened her mouth.

Hayden let go of the headboard and dropped down onto all fours so that his hard cock was just above her mouth and his face was above her pussy. "You can start now," he said harshly as he bent this elbows and lowered himself. "Put your head back. I want to make sure you can take all of me."

She followed his instruction, positioning her head so that her wide-open mouth was directly below his jutting shaft. He lowered his hips just far enough to dip the tip of his dick into her mouth. He lifted it out. "That's right." He slid his tongue between her slick nether lips, then straightened his arms, lifting himself so that he hovered above her. "If you do a good job, I'll eat your pussy."

Rachelle started to speak, but he cut her off. "Remember the rules."

She remained silent, opening her mouth again, readying herself to suck his dick. He lowered his hips and gradually slid his cock in. She closed her lips around his shaft and sucked, pulling him deeper and deeper in. Once he was in as far as he could go, she curved her tongue around his shaft, swirling it around him with careful attention.

"That's right. Just like that."

His encouragement made her suck harder, and he let himself go, forgetting about the thing watching him and feeling nothing except the strong pull of Rachelle's mouth as she sucked and licked his rock-hard dick. The simmering current surging through his body got hotter, heating his muscles, centering his attention on his own needs. The intensity was frightening, the urge to brutally fuck her mouth nearly overwhelming. To fight the all-consuming lust, he bent down and licked Rachelle's pussy. Her folds were soft and so, so wet. Her clit was stiff and easy to find. He flicked his tongue across it and her thighs tensed. She lifted her hips, asking for more. Hayden responded to her need, sliding his tongue in deeper, caressing her clit gently, over and over again. She matched his rhythm, licking and sucking his cock, using her mouth to consume his shaft.

He delved deeper, and again she responded, using her mouth to tell him she wanted more. Each time he stroked, she did, and their motions became one.

The bliss was short lived. His awareness of Mattie came back, slipping into the back of his mind, then seeping into his consciousness. His awareness of her flowed through him like a heavy fog, filling his veins with thick dread. He fought it, trying to concentrate on the slick folds of Rachelle's pussy, gliding his tongue over her sensitive skin, but the heavy pulse of his blood slowed his senses. He could no longer feel the glide of Rachelle's tongue on his cock or the wet heat of her mouth on his skin.

Hayden looked up and *she* was there, staring at him, consuming him with her greedy gaze and demanding him to give in to her. He did. With his next breath, his senses tripled. He could see the flecks in Mattie's eyes. Somehow, impossibly, he smelled her icy scent, felt her breath inside him. The sensations from the flick of Rachelle's tongue and the slick heat of her mouth returned. Keeping his gaze connected with Mattie's, he thrust deeply into Rachelle's throat. His motions turned careless, but she didn't pull away. Instead, she took still more of him, letting him fuck her mouth with harsh jerks.

Every nerve ending in his body fired. His cock twitched and his balls tightened. Hayden felt it all, every tiny motion of Rachelle's tongue, the slight graze of her teeth, the fleshy curves of the inside of her mouth, and even the whisper of her breath brushing across the fine hairs circling the base of his cock. The sensations pooled together, creating a wave of hot electricity that ran through his body, electrifying his muscles and heating his blood. It was like nothing he'd ever experienced, let alone imagined.

Mattie owned him. But God help him, right then he didn't care. He would've done anything to keep the wicked sensation alive and breathing inside him—an all-consuming life force of its own. He dropped his head to taste Rachelle's pussy, sucked her plump flesh into his mouth, then speared her clit with his tongue. Each lick brought a new wave of unbelievable, impossible pleasure, and Rachelle's response told him she felt the same ferocious electricity and all-consuming unnatural bliss. Hayden lifted his head.

As he locked gazes with the creature, Rachelle sucked his cock, swirling her tongue around his stiff shaft. Mattie knew each spin of Rachelle's tongue. Knew how desperately the girl beneath him was sucking, doing her best to satisfy him. She nodded and lowered her palm from the window.

He dropped his head, again placing his open mouth across Rachelle's hot, wet pussy and sucking gently, pulling her nether lips into his mouth. His mouth came alive with her sweetness, and she responded by angling her head back to slide his rod deeper down the back of her throat. She took all of him, her lips brushing the skin at the base of his shaft.

The sensation was as awesome as it was undeniable, unbelievable. Hayden gave himself up to the pleasure and pumped his hips, lifting his dick out of her mouth then thrusting it back in.

His cock twitched, and the first spurt of his hot cum rolled down the back of Rachelle's throat. She kept him in, widening even more, letting him fuck her mouth as hard and fast as he could. Somehow he managed to keep his mouth on her pussy, zeroing in on her clit. Her release came with a hard tremor, making her legs tense and her back lift off the bed. He thrust and jerked. She stilled and gave her body over to him. They melted together, becoming one explosion of sex.

Even after the tremors faded, he lay across her, she licking his dick and he licking her pussy. The small, tender flicks of her tongue started to bring blood back into his shaft. She licked him several more times then pulled away. His dick still ached for attention.

"Can I talk now?" she asked, putting a crack in the brutal, sensual spell.

Hayden gave her thigh one last lick, then rolled off her. He raised himself up and twisted to see her face. Her eyes were half-closed and her mouth glistened. "What?"

"I'm not sure that counts as fucking."

Hayden spun all the way around and crawled forward so his face was just above hers. "You don't feel...what?"

"I felt it. It's just that, well," she lifted her body and nudged his dick with her hip, "I noticed you're still a bit stiff, and it would be a shame to waste that ready cock."

Despite the mind-blowing orgasm, his dick was

getting hard again and the need to fuck still pulsed through his veins. He ached for release with an angry, unnatural desperation and there was only one way to get it. He rubbed himself against Rachelle and as she purred a pang of guilt vibrated through him. What he'd just done to her was dishonest. He'd used her and he was about to use her again. How many more times after that? Hayden untied her wrists, slid his hands beneath her, then spun her so she was diagonal across the bed. This time he would have to be just short of cruel.

Once she was settled, he worked his way down her body, providing a show for the creature outside, running a row of kisses from behind Rachelle's neck to between her breasts. The stockings had held and her tits were high and tight. He pulled one hard tip into his mouth, grabbed the other with his hand and pinched the nipple. She rolled her shoulders and spread her legs. He positioned his shaft between her wet pussy lips. She was so slick, so ready for him. His cock was hard, his entire body stiff and tense. With one solid thrust he filled her tight channel then paused, taking the time to feel her tightness squeezing his shaft.

He whispered into her ear. "That what you had in mind?"

She moaned. "Fuck me, Hayden." She lifted her hips, shifted her legs to spread them even wider, and grabbed his shoulders. Squeezing her fingers deep into his muscles, she groaned. "Now. Do it."

Again, Mattie's breath slipped inside him, an evil vapor that dazed his mind. He lifted his body and angled himself for a fierce, hard swing. He drove into Rachelle's core, but unlike the first time, didn't wait for her body to adjust to his cock. He hammered into

41

her tight body with feral thrusts, pounding and grinding against her pelvis, feeling every curve of her cunt, even the slight tickle of the dark-brown hairs between her legs. The action of fucking was demanding, stealing the last shreds of control he had over his own body. His sense of time and place fell away and long hollow seconds stole his consciousness as his body swirled and tumbled into pitch-black darkness. The nothingness was both brilliant and terrifying. He hung there, in the abyss, teetering on consciousness.

By the time the first wave of his orgasm grabbed him, Hayden had forgotten the woman beneath him. After the jerks of his cock subsided, and his awareness returned, he rolled off Rachelle and pressed his palm to her stomach. Her eyes were closed, her breathing jagged. He didn't even know if she'd come.

He lifted himself, unbound her breasts. After he tossed the stockings to the floor, he pulled her to him and kissed her moist neck. A bead of sweat rolled down, leaving a trail between her breasts. The drop crossed over the red mark left behind by the binding. Outside the window, gusts of snow brushed the glass, swirling in circles under the yellow light of street lamps.

Beside him, Rachelle stirred. "You did, in fact, fuck me senseless." She set her hands across his, laced her fingers through his and squeezed them lightly. "I'm not even sure I remember all of it." She tilted her head and looked up at him from under her lashes. "Sounds crazy. Unbelievable. Doesn't it?"

He lifted their laced hands. "You liked it?"

"Liked it? Shit. I don't know." She took her hands

back, sat up, and looked out the window. "Maybe it's the storm, but I— I—"

"Me too," he cut her off intentionally. Whatever they'd just experienced, he didn't want to dissect, to analyze.

Both their bodies were covered in salty sweat, slick from Rachelle's arousal and his come. He pressed a kiss to her neck and slid away, then climbed out of bed and threw the cover over her, shielding her naked body from view. Once he was satisfied that she was covered, he slipped down the hall and into the bathroom.

A burst of snow-filled wind swirled into the small room, carrying a bitter chill. The window was open and her scent filled the room. Hayden dropped his hand from the light switch, leaving the room dim and bracing as the sensual dread settled in the back of his mouth. Mattie pressed her cold, damp body against him, shoved him to the wall. Behind her, over her shoulder, he saw their reflection in the mirror above the sink. Ice and snow clung to her tangled hair, dripping onto the solid curves of her back and shoulders. The sections of her bare skin glowed. Between the strips of cloth, he spotted a wide column of black ink staring at the base of her spine and ending about halfway up her back.

Even after the show he'd put on for her, coming twice in less than an hour, his cock stirred when she pressed herself against him, grinding her pelvis against his. The damp strips of red wool rubbed across his nipples and they tightened into pointed peaks. How was it possible to be aroused yet again?

It wasn't. None of this was.

"Well done, researcher." She grabbed his cock

and curved her fingers around his hardening shaft. "You impress me."

There were no human words for what he was feeling. He grunted in response, but his body betrayed him, and he found himself leaning toward her, seeking her strength and giving in to the power she had over him.

"You know, with only a bit of encouragement, she'll be ready to go again too."

Hayden shook his head, even though his dick was growing still larger in her palm. "No," he said. "I've had enough."

"You've had enough when I say you've had enough." She let go of his shaft and reached around to grab his ass. "Maybe if I join you two, you'll feel differently." She caressed his flesh, sliding her hand between his ass cheeks. "I'd be happy to—"

"Take control. I know." He tried to push her back but she used her strength to hold him.

"That's right." She nudged his chin with her nose. "You're beginning to understand how our relationship works."

He tried again to push her away and she grabbed his arms, spun them both around, lifted him, and set him on the edge of the sink. She tapped the door with her foot and it slid closed.

"You and I are a matched set. A linked pair. Unless, of course..." she tipped her head toward the bedroom, "I decide to add her. Then we'll be a trio. I like the sound of that. I've never had two servicing me at the same time."

The hard edge of the sink cut into the back of Hayden's thighs. "Leave Rachelle out of this," he said, ignoring the pain in his legs as he shoved at her.

"She has a lot of spunk." She held on to him and whispered into his ear. "I think I like her."

Hayden stopped struggling. "You don't know her."

"And you do? Are you sure about that? I think we both learned a lot about her tonight. She's... responsive." Mattie let go of his arms and set her palms on his inner thighs, just inches from his jutting shaft. "I like responsive."

Hayden's was dick hard and ready for fucking, and he knew if she wanted, she could demand it from him. And he would do it. He'd do whatever she wanted. He worked to keep the fearful dread out of his eyes when he lifted his face.

She moved her hands in and brushed her icy fingertips across his ball sac. An electric pulse shot up from his groin. The muscles of his torso twitched.

"I don't need you again. Yet. But it's good to know I've chosen well." She glanced at his cock. "The others will be jealous."

"Others?"

She grinned as she caressed the hard edges of his shaft. "The others in the tribe."

The tribe. Images flickered in his mind. The sex rituals, the man tied to the tree, the undeads constant need for sex. Bile rose in Haydn's throat, burning an evil path up from his gut.

"Don't look like that. It's good to make people jealous." She pressed a kiss to his neck. "Sometimes, anyway. And especially some people. The ones who deserve it."

Maybe that was true. But they weren't talking about *people*.

She kissed his neck again, softer, letting her cold

45

lips linger on his still-feverish flesh. Each press gave new life to the sexual pull she had over him. A pull Hayden did not want or understand.

"I have to get back to Rachelle," he said, speaking softly. He leaned back and caught Mattie's gaze. "Alone."

She stilled, no longer the aggressor, but not ready to let him go either. That same expression passed over her face, the one he'd seen outside when she pressed her hand to the window. The vulnerability was a surprise, a shock, but somehow it made sense. She must have been human once. What was she like then? Hayden shoved the question aside.

He set his hands on her waist and kissed her lightly on her cold mouth. "It'll be better this way." He didn't really know what he meant by the comment, but it sounded right. And it kept her from reaching for him again.

"Better for who?" she asked, her voice small and thin and surprisingly unsure.

"For you. Me. Rachelle." Again he wasn't sure what he meant, but as he spoke he got the sense that it wasn't the words she was after. It was the exchange. A conversation. For the first time since they'd met, he had the upper hand. If he kept it, he could get her to do what he wanted. He nodded toward the open window. "It'll be good this way. You go back out the way you came. She won't see you."

He touched her face, pulling her toward him. He kissed her again, lightly, just a whisper of lips, then gently turned her toward the window.

She let go of him, took one step back, then another toward the window. "I'm leaving because I want to," she said, raking over his naked body with her careful study.

He nodded as he gradually slid off the sink. "I know," he replied, rubbing the pain out of the backs of his legs.

"Hayden?"

It was Rachelle, the soft pad of her feet getting louder as she approached the closed bathroom door.

Mattie slid silently to the window, moving without taking her gaze from his bare skin.

Hayden turned on the faucet and spoke loudly over the rush of the water. "I'll be right there."

"You okay?" Rachelle called from the hallway. "Everything okay?" She was right on the other side of the door.

"I said I'll be right there. Go back to bed where you belong."

He heard her laugh, a husky warm sound. "Okay, all right. I get it," she called, her voice growing distant as she headed back to the bedroom. "But you don't have to be so bossy about it."

"You like me bossy," he yelled, forcing lightness into his voice.

Mattie was pushing the sash of the window all the way up. Once the opening was wide enough for her to climb through, she sat on the ledge and swung her legs over. She turned and looked at him from over her shoulder. "You'll see me again soon. You know that, right?"

He nodded, staring into the swirling steam rising up from the sink. When he finally lifted his head, she was gone, out into the endless storm, and the window had been pulled shut. Except for the evil electricity coursing through him and the last vestiges of her scent, it was as though she'd never been there.

Hayden grabbed a towel from the rack and set it in the sink. Hot water splashed across it, soaking it quickly. Once it was completely wet, he turned off the water, wrung it out, then wrapped it into another towel and carried them both to the bedroom. Rachelle was under the covers, only her face visible above the quilt. The sexual haze was gone from her eyes, and she was smiling.

Weighed down by the guilt over what he'd gotten her in to, Hayden climbed onto the bed and pulled the covers from her body. She was still naked, and the firm outline of her body was outlined by the shadowy light coming in through the now-vacant window.

"See something you like?" she asked.

Hayden took the hot, wet towel from inside the dry one. "I like it so much I want to take good care of it."

"I thought you already did."

Hayden turned away and pressed the corner of the steaming, damp towel to the top arch of her foot. "Is it too warm?"

She stretched her legs and placed her feet side by side. "You may proceed."

He took his time, working gradually up the insides of her thighs, then circling around her pelvis. By the time he wiped the moisture off with the dry towel, she'd fallen asleep. He tossed both towels across his laundry basket and climbed in beside her. Outside, the wind-filled snow continued and the wind howled. Icy flakes brushed the windowpane.

Hayden rolled over and tried to concentrate on the

curves of Rachelle's shoulders and the sexy slope of her neck. He set his hand on her throat and felt the light, steady beat of her pulse.

He couldn't do that again. He had to get rid of Mattie.

He rolled over, trying not to think about what she'd done to him in the bathroom—lifting him up, setting him on the edge of the sink. Owning him with her emotionless caress. His cock responding to her touch—even when he didn't want it to. A shiver worked up from the soles of his feet, the rousing tremor, a mixture of fear and sexual need. It wasn't right to feel this way. It wasn't human. And there wasn't anyone alive who could help him.

Unless someone else had been where he'd been and knew what he needed to know.

He wasn't Mattie's first. He did his best to quell the roll in his stomach as he accepted what he'd become. A toy. A necessary pet. A sexual servant.

What had become of the others who filled the role before him?

Killed? Or worse, did they become like her, a creature that preyed on others?

If she hadn't come in through the library window when she had, interrupting the research he'd been doing for the newspaper, maybe he'd have the answers. He'd know what to do to protect himself or at least how to keep Rachelle safe. Hayden tossed again, turning away from the storm and the thing that lurked in it.

No, not a thing.

Things.

Chapter Four

"You've had enough when I say you've had enough."

"It's fantastic stuff. You're going to get more of it, kid."

Hayden cringed at the word *kid*. Holding the phone to his ear, he hopped off the curb and leapt over a snow bank, offering his reply as he stomped across the nearly empty street. "This whole zombie thing is going to blow over. The snow will melt, the comic convention will end, and everyone will get back to their life and forget about zombie tribes and life-or-death sex."

"Life-or-death sex. I love it! Get that down, use it for the next headline."

Hayden reached the corner and jumped over another pile of snow. "There doesn't have to be another headline."

"What's your problem, college boy? You too good for zombies?"

Not by a long shot, apparently.

"This is the best angle we've had in months and you know it. Get your ass back over to the library right now, or wherever you dug that stuff up, and write me something about that life-or-death sex. And more pictures. I want more of those."

Images of the previous night slashed through Hayden's mind as Bob continued. "You do this for me, I'll do something for you."

Hayden halted in the middle of the sidewalk. He'd never heard that, or anything close to it, come out of Keeler's mouth. "I'll look into it tomorrow."

"Tomorrow?"

"Yeah, I'm all the way over in Cambridge," he lied, then continued with the truth. "I spent hours talking to that widow you set me up with. I got some useable stuff. Papers that prove she's the long-lost daughter of Punchy McLaughlin."

"All right. Fine. That does sound choice. But I want you back on the zombie sex stuff first thing in the morning. Don't even come in to the office. Just get your ass out of bed then get me something hot. And fresh. You know I want it *fresh*."

"Yeah. I know." After Bob grunted a goodbye, Hayden ended the call but didn't slide his phone into his pocket.

He started walking again, making a list of things he wanted from Keeler. Money. A better desk. But most of all access to the man's connections. Even though he ran a tabloid, Keeler knew people at *The Globe* and a few at *The Times*—people who could offer him a better job. A real job. An introduction to a couple of them, that's what he wanted most.

The streets were amazingly clear and the snow had stopped that morning, but the going was still slow and his legs ached from stepping over uneven heaps all day. Once he was on Commonwealth, a block from his apartment, he stopped, leaned on a low wall sheltering some steps and hit Rachelle's number.

She answered on the first ring. Her greeting was the usual, but the tone in her voice made the hair on the back of his neck rise.

"You okay?" he asked. "Something going on?"

"Going on?" She laughed, then added, "What would be going on?"

He scanned the nearby rooftops and checked under the eaves. "You sound...different."

Her laugh lowered, the sound making a shiver roll down his back. "I have you to thank for that."

More images from the night before tumbled through his mind. Some good. Most not. "So everything's okay?"

"Stop with that already. When will you be home?"

"Soon." He watched a van from Cindy's Market drive past, another lie forming as he started to speak. "Hey, I'm expecting a package. You didn't happen to see a delivery person hanging around out front, or anyone looking for me, or knocking on the door, anything like that, did you?"

"No. Hurry up and get home."

Hayden kicked a clump of snow. It rolled a few inches then hit another. There was so much snow. It was everywhere, piled high and stacked in corners. And the wind, constant and biting. There was no escaping. "I am on the way, but I have to write up an interview and do...some other stuff when I get there."

"Other stuff, huh?" She laughed tightly, the sound rolled through him, making his muscles twitch.

Rachelle ignored both his comment and the silence. "Come over to my place as soon as you get home."

"I—"

She interrupted him with *bye now* and clicked off. He slipped his phone into his pocket. Overheard, the sun slid behind a cloud and the street dimmed. Off to the west, a new bank of clouds hung in the sky, the edges an ashy gray, the centers dark. More snow. A lot more. A blue pickup passed, its tires making a hushed rumble as it turned away and headed toward the river. A yellow Brookline Cab Company van sat at the corner, its light on, a stream of exhaust chugging out the back. The thin trail of the cabbie's cigarette dangling out the open driver's side window spiraled up toward the darkening sky. The cabbie turned, catching Hayden's gaze as he took a long draw. The man didn't look away as he flicked the butt out onto the street. The window went up and the van rumbled off.

Hayden pushed away from the wall. When he reached his place, he scanned the rooftops and checked under the eaves. Empty. He jogged up the steps, swung open the door. Nothing. But he wasn't dumb enough to think she wasn't around. He could sense her, feel her deep inside his body, thrumming in his blood. She would show up, and there was nothing he could do to avoid it. The best he could hope for was to be ready, brace himself for her effect on him and, most of all, keep Rachelle away.

Once he reached the top landing, he paused to slide his feet out of his snow-covered boots and set them by the wall. He dug out his keys and reached forward to put the key in the lock, but the door swung open slightly, enough for him to see the outline of Rachelle's body. No fur coat this time. She was wearing a ratty Boston College sweatshirt, jeans and red wool socks.

She swung the door open, grabbed his arm and pulled him in. He stumbled, his stocking feet sliding on the wood floors. "Surprise, your friend from work was looking for you."

"Hey there, Hayden."

Mattie. On his couch, smug as ever. Everything about her was the same, except for the addition of a black leather jacket, zipped up high, completely covering her breasts.

"Wipe that look off your face." She leaned back, arching her back as she crossed her bare legs. "I didn't break in or anything. Your girlfriend found me sitting on the steps. She's a sweetie, so she let me in. If it weren't for her, I might be hiding under an eave, you know, just trying to keep warm." She slid a smile over at Rachelle. "Your girl and I have been getting acquainted and I've been filling her in on everything."

Hayden pulled in a breath and the scent—icy, metallic, unavoidable—rippled through him, nearly knocking him off balance.

"Why didn't you tell me you were going to keep working on the zombie stuff?" Rachelle swept around the room to stand next to the couch, two feet from Mattie. "It sounds awesome."

"I— I—"

Mattie cocked her head and ran her palm down her leg. "Did Bob tell you to keep it a secret?"

Hayden turned away from them, using the time it took to set down his book bag and take off his coat to get himself together.

"I can't believe you didn't tell Rachelle anything at all about our research," Mattie said.

"*Our* research?"

54

Rachelle came around to Hayden's side. "Mattie told me some about it, it's, it's—"

"Sexy," Mattie cut in, stretching out the word with a low husky growl.

Rachelle pulled on the hem of her sweatshirt as she glanced at Mattie. "That too, for sure. I was going to say, kind of creepy." She glanced at Mattie. "But in a fun way."

Hayden watched Rachelle continue to tug on her sweatshirt, her gaze cast down as her fingers played with the edge. What happened to that sexual machine from last night? What was with the coy act? He dropped into the chair across from the couch. "Creepy but fun?"

Mattie pointed a pale finger at Hayden. "I found one of those zombie tribes you were telling me about. Well, actually I didn't find it, so I haven't seen it yet, but someone I know—and trust—told me about it. He saw it." She dug into her coat pocket and pulled out a wadded-up sheet of brown paper that looked like a piece of a brown grocery bag. She flattened it against her knees. "A guy named Matthew gave this to me. We should go check it out."

Hayden's stomach clenched as Mattie pushed the map into Rachelle's hand. Rachelle lifted the brown paper, her eyebrows twisting as she looked over the scribbled lines drawn with black and blue marker. She flattened it across her legs and leaned closer. "How far away is it?"

"About 40 minutes," Mattie replied.

"Rachelle? Do you actually think there's a tribe of zombies camped out near here?" Hayden inflected his voice with disbelief. "That's ridiculous."

"It sounds fun, Hayden. Let's go check it out." She ran her fingertips along the paper's edge. "What else do we have to do?"

"You want to go look for zombies? Seriously?"

Mattie unzipped her jacket, exposing the highest of the red wool straps binding her breasts. "If you don't want to go, Hayden, the three of us could stay here. I'm sure we could find something to do."

A wave of feral lust so intense it made him nauseous rolled through him.

Rachelle's attention stayed riveted to the paper in her hands. "I know there's no such thing as zombies, but the map looks amazing." She waved it at Hayden. "Maybe it's a bunch of people pretending to be zombies, that'd be great for you. You could take more pictures. Ask them questions. Bob would love that, right?"

Yes, he would.

But Hayden did not want Rachelle pulled in any deeper. This was his problem. Not hers. And since when was she so concerned about his job? "The roads are too bad to drive."

"They're fine. I got here, didn't I?" Mattie unzipped her jacket another inch. The swells of her breasts showed above the zipper. "Or would you rather stay in?"

Rachelle flopped back into the cushions, her face a mask of petulance. "I don't want to stay here. I want to see the camp. Whatever it is." Before he could come up with something to stop the idea, she rolled off the couch, stood. "We'll take your car, Hayden. That's why you have four-wheel drive, to do this sort of investigative journalism. Right?" Her phone started to buzz, so she dug into her purse and pulled it out. "It's Daddy," she said, then turned away to answer it.

Hayden stood. "I need a drink."

"Put a kettle on," Mattie called after him. "We can take some tea on the drive."

Hayden walked to the kitchen, heading straight for his bourbon. He didn't bother with a glass. Three swallows later, Mattie came up beside him, surrounding him with her ice-cold scent. "You know we're going." She slipped over to the stove, picked up the kettle, shook it, then moved to the sink to fill it.

Hayden took another swig then put the bottle away.

She set the kettle on to boil then leaned on the counter, staring at him, green glimmer fogging her eyes. She unzipped her coat the rest of the way, pushed it open. She ran her fingertips across her nipples, making them peak beneath the red wool. When Hayden looked up from her breasts, her gaze was on his crotch.

"Like I said before," she murmured, "we're done when I say we're done."

"What happens when we're done? To me?" Hayden spoke over the bits of Rachelle's conversation that drifted into the kitchen from the other room.

Mattie continued moving her fingertips across her breasts, playing with her nipples. "If I were you, I guess I'd want to know that too."

"So tell me," he asked, trying to ignore the truth that his cock was already hard.

She leaned forward and whispered, "Well, you see, it kind of depends."

He shifted. "On what?"

A bright flash of green passed through in her eyes. Hayden winced from the pain of his own excitement.

"You know I'm not wearing any panties, right?" She smirked, then leaned back and crossed her arms right underneath her breasts, shoved them up, her tight nipples straining against the fabric. One quick tug and those breasts would be in full view.

"On what?" he asked again.

A hard smile pulled on her mouth then she mouthed, *no panties.*

Of course she wasn't going to answer his question. *Bitch.*

Hayden did his best to ignore her comment, but the image of her bare pussy wouldn't leave. "Fine." He shrugged, accepting the inevitable. "Let's go. Follow your fucking map." Hayden pulled his gaze away from Mattie's body as he called into the other room. "Rachelle, you sure you want to do this?"

There was a pause in her phone conversation, then, she called back. "What, are you kidding? Of course."

Mattie pulled her coat closed then moved to the hall and tipped her head around the corner. "Do you have some real boots, Rachelle? A heavy coat?" She cut her gaze to Hayden, winked, then added, "It's going to be really cold and we'll probably have to walk through some woods. Don't want you to be uncomfortable or anything like that."

Rachelle's reply, *Good idea, thanks. I'll be back in a few* was followed more pieces of her phone conversation and the beat of her feet across the wood floors. The phone conversation faded.

As soon as the door slammed shut, Mattie's coat

was on the floor, and she was on him, grabbing his belt, her pale hands a blur. When her fingers tangled, he unbuckled it. With one motion, she shoved his pants and briefs down. She grabbed his dick, caressed it, gently running her cold fingers up and down his warm skin. "If you hurry, she won't have to walk in on us."

The kettle's shrill scream sounded. Hayden scrambled to shut off the flame. The kettle continued to scream until he pushed it off the burner. "Turn around."

Pivoting on the toes of her boots, she looked over her shoulder. "That's more like it, library boy."

"Don't call me that." He lifted her skirt and positioned his cock between her ass cheeks. "Hold on to the counter."

Without worrying about whether or not he hurt her, he impaled her with a single sharp drive. She was tight, but her body accepted his full, hard length. He backed out and plunged in again. She bucked, encouraging him to pound into her and he did, feeling the hard muscles of her ass with each drive. Flickers of the constant sexual fire that she'd lit in him flamed and tore through his limbs in a fierce and angry blaze. He pumped his dick into her pussy with quick, remorseless thrusts, grabbing her hips, digging his fingers into her cool flesh. His cock got bigger, his sac tight, and she grunted as he ground into her.

Tremors rolled over her body, and he felt the walls of her vagina squeeze, starting to pull the cum from his dick. The last few thrusts were vicious and fierce, almost to the point of pain, but he couldn't control himself, didn't really want to, and he fell into the dark bliss of the mind-numbing physical release. The pleasure died as quickly as it begun.

He withdrew, pulled down her skirt, then adjusted his own clothes.

A few seconds of his life, that was all the time it had been. That's what he told himself, but he knew it was more.

Mattie looked him up and down as she adjusted the bindings covering her breasts. That green hue, gone. But for how long?

"You made a mess of me," she said, pretending to tug wrinkles from the pleats of her skirt. "Well done, researcher."

Resentment rolled through him, bitterness followed. "Why do you keep calling me that?" he asked, getting past her.

She picked up her jacket and followed him into the living room. "That's what you do, isn't it? Research."

"I write for a tabloid newspaper." He ran his fingers through his hair, wondering if Rachelle would be able to tell what they'd been doing while she was getting boots. He looked at Mattie, and added, "That's not research."

She kicked the back of his calf, and he stumbled until he grabbed the edge of the couch.

"You're so smart, Hayden," she said after a husky laugh. "I can't believe you haven't figured it out."

He looked over his shoulder at her.

"What I want from you," she said.

He pointed to his dick, then moved as far from her as possible, stopping beside the picture window that looked out onto the street. Snow and ice, heaped everywhere, covering everything. There were a few signs of the city coming back to life, cars, store lights, but it was apparent Boston was still in the clutches of a nasty storm. A life-squelching blizzard.

She zipped up her jacket and folded her arms across her chest, a sold wall of stealth and wickedness. "A man like you, with so much to offer a woman and you think fucking is all I want?"

He stared out at the night. Rows of white lights blinked back at him. Snow lay heaped in corners, heavy and dense, turning into shadows as the sun set on the slow-moving city. "I don't care what you want," he said, watching yet another plow shove its way down the street.

"You ought to."

Rachelle swung into the room, the giant fur wrapped around her body, Bean boots swinging beneath the hem. "You guys aren't ready?" She glanced between them, hers bright, a fresh coat of red sheen on her eager lips.

Mattie swept over and shoved Hayden toward the hall, fake laughing. It was all a game. "Get ready, Hayden." She wrapped her arm around Rachelle's shoulders, kissed her on top of the head, then took her hand to lead her to the kitchen. "I'll make us some tea and make sure everything is taken care of out here."

The sight of the two of them, hand in hand, narrowed Hayden's focus to only two things. Getting what he wanted—something fresh to give Bob so he could get that something in return—and what he needed—a way to erase Mattie from of his and Rachelle's life.

61

Chapter Five
"Well done, researcher."

Hayden opened his eyes and watched his breath come out in frigid puffs. The stream of fog hung in the air, evaporating slowly as it drifted upward. Beyond his car's windshield, moonlight blended into a distant narrow line of snow-heaped trees, stretching across the horizon. The sky was clear, the night still, the air bitter with an icy scent.

Metallic and sharp as a knife.

In the seat beside him, someone groaned, low and husky. He forced his eyes to focus as he moved his head.

Rachelle, wrapped in her fur coat, opened her eyes. "Oh, hey."

He nodded, fighting a wave of dizziness and struggling to gain full consciousness

"Guess I feel asleep." She rubbed the fogged up window with her mittened hands, her head pivoting to take in the wide, snow-covered field surrounding the small turnout where they were parked. "Are we near the tribe?"

Obviously, he'd been out too. He grabbed the steering wheel to pull himself upright. "Not sure."

Mattie lingered outside, her black boots feet deep

down in the white snow, the wind pushing her skirt against her thighs.

Rachelle dropped her hands, her laughter creating a misty cloud. "You drove us here. How do you not know where we are?"

Hayden glanced at the backseat. His backpack with his notebook, camera and tablet was there, the bag of food they'd brought and the thermos. The was the last thing he remembered—Mattie giving him directions while they were all drinking the tea she'd made right before they left. He patted his chest pocket. His phone was gone. He reached back, checking his back pocket, feeling for his wallet and noticed his belt was undone, hanging down the back of his pants.

"What's wrong?" Rachelle asked.

"Nothing. Let's get out." He shoved open the car door and climbed out, fixing his belt as he stood. A wave of dizziness found him and he grabbed the top of the door, gulping in some of the frigid air as he watched Rachelle move away from the car.

Mattie trudged over, her boots breaking the quiet with soft thuds. "The effects will wear off once you start moving."

He pulled his sweater over his belt. "Seems I've already been doing some moving."

Her gaze lingered on his hands as she shrugged. "You did a little. I did more."

"What was in that tea?" he asked, lowering his voice and moving closer.

She kicked snow at him. "Pissed that you don't remember fucking me while your girlfriend was passed out in the next seat?"

The pang of guilt for getting Rachelle involved

with this vile horror show wasn't surprising so even though that was there, it wasn't remorse that made him wince. It was the fear of how much worse this shit could get. He looked back at the snow-packed road, then took in the field glowing under the moonlight, the trees in the distance, before turning back to his car with the fogged up windows.

"Don't worry Hayden. It's perfectly safe to drive while under the influence. It doesn't," she glanced at his crotch, "impair you. But it does block your memory, so I actually did you a favor." She leaned in to whisper, "You can thank me later." Her scent, more of a sensation rather than an actual smell, filled his nostrils, creating a scratch in the back of his throat. Fresh blood, that's what her scent reminded him of. That bitter iron tang. He swallowed to avoid gagging and backed up.

Rachelle was spinning in circles, her arms wide, her face toward the sky. "It's so dark out here. All the stars!" She stopped twirling and focused on Mattie as she stomped through the snow to stand closer to her and Hayden. "Where are we, anyway?"

Mattie lifted the map and pointed to the top right corner. "We'll walk up the river, through these trees where the snow isn't as deep. Then, once we get there, we work our way around this section here." She pointed to what looked to be dense cluster of pines then slid her finger to the X. After holding it up for a few more seconds, she rolled it up and tucked it into her leather. "No problem. We'll get there in less than an hour."

She wasn't going to answer the question about where they actually were. If she'd wanted them to know that, she wouldn't have drugged them with whatever the hell she'd put in the tea. Hayden zipped his coat then propped his foot on the bumper and listened. Nothing. Not a single sound. There was no telling how long they'd been driving or what there was, or wasn't, nearby. "Just leave the car here?"

"Like Mattie said. We won't be gone long. A couple hours, that's it." Rachelle spun again, moving so fast that her scarf flew out, waving through the frigid night air like a banner.

Mattie opened the car door, took Hayden's bag then held it out for him. "You'll want this."

He dropped the strap across his shoulder. Mattie tugged on it to pull out the thermos. Hayden's stomach rolled as she tucked the bottle under her arm.

Rachelle rounded the back of the car and tucked herself between Mattie and Hayden. The three of them stood shoulder to shoulder, searching into the night until Rachelle broke the dense, cold silence. "You really think we're going to see something out there?"

"My friend must've seen something or else he wouldn't have made the map. Right?" Mattie broke away, started walking toward the trees.

Rachelle followed, her shorter legs working harder to get through the snow.

Filled with dread, Hayden moved forward.

Once the three of them were shoulder to shoulder again, Rachelle turned to Hayden. He felt the weight of her stare but avoided making eye contact until she grabbed his arm, forcing him to look over. "It's not anything dangerous, is it? I mean, nothing bad can happen to us, right?"

Mattie bumped Rachelle's arm. "Only bad stuff

we want to happen." She glanced over her shoulder and caught Hayden's gaze. "Right, Hayden?"

He jerked his gaze away, but out of the corner of his eye he saw her unscrew the top of the thermos. She passed it to Rachelle. She drank. Rachelle passed it to him. Still walking, he looked down into the dark hole.

"It'll warm you up," Rachelle said.

"Yeah." Mattie added, leering at him over the top of Rachelle's head. Wind was pushing snow through the air, and the messy stands of her hair were starting to clump with snow. Flakes were clinging to her lashes and wetting her icy mouth. She pressed her lips together and lifted her chin to look down her nose at him. "You want it. Don't you?"

It wasn't about what he wanted.

And so he lifted the thermos, put his mouth above the black hole and drank.

* * *

The dizziness of coming to was more intense this time. Hayden opened his eyes, strained to focus. There was nothing but blurry lines and faded colors—brown, white, and beige. Move, he reminded himself, get it to wear off. He breathed deep and stretched his arms along his sides, flexing his muscles, and sliding his hands downward as he arched his back. In the distance, a chain rattled. He braced his hands and tried to lift himself. Again, the sound of metal on metal, closer this time. Fighting a thickness in his mind, he pushed harder to get himself upright. The reward was a sharp snap to his neck, a shooting pain down his back, and the same sound—louder. He reached up, his fingers curled around a ring circling his neck. He tugged, rough steel cut into his palms and there was more rattling.

"Rachelle?" He crawled backwards to create slack, sat upright then yelled her name again. His vision was clearing, he saw bare log walls, a window framed with a shabby muslin curtain, and a solid wood door. Blinking to gain more clarity, he struggled to search the small cabin room as he called her name again.

Nothing.

He dropped back, closed his eyes, fighting the guilt as he dug back through his memory.

"She's fine. Probably having the best time she's had in a while." Mattie emerged from a corner, her eyes glowing green. "Except for last night, I mean. That was exceptional, wasn't it?"

She sat on the edge of the bed, lantern light from a table casting shadows on her face, and threw back the brown blanket, exposing him. He was naked, his cock partially erect. "Your girlfriend is both curious and enthusiastic. A very, very nice combination." She ran her cool fingers up his shaft. The muscles of his thighs twitched and more blood flooded to his dick.

"You're enthusiastic too." She looked up. "Lucky for me, I don't care whether or not you admit it."

Hayden gritted his teeth against the want curling through him, heating his cock and reminding him how it felt to thrust into Mattie's icy body. He turned away, tensed against the sensations. His vision was clearing, but very few memories were coming back.

Beyond the edge of the bed, in the corner opposite the one where Mattie had been, fire brightened a squat wood stove. Two cast iron pots hung from ceiling hooks. About three feet from the stove was a square table with two wooden chairs. The window was above the table, but there was nothing visible except a smooth blackness—a never-ending night. Mattie continued staring at him, her eyes flickering, mouth softer than usual. And her scent. It was there too, coating Hayden's skin like a fine mist.

"You know." She smiled, moving her gaze back to his eyes. "I think I forgot to thank you. I told you to make it good, give me something worth watching, and you did." She stroked his balls, causing a shiver to rip upward from his crotch. "I appreciated your effort."

The shiver continued upward, into his chest. "I didn't do it for you."

She continued caressing him. "I was part of it, though. Wasn't I?"

Hot flames of fierce hunger flared deep. There was no point in denying what she already knew to be true, so he nodded. She opened her mouth, laid her palm across her lips, then licked her hand several times with the full length of her tongue. She jerked her hand up and down, then bent to lick the tip. It was then that he realized he was beginning to crave that icy wetness, the unique chill of her mouth. Her hair brushed his thigh as she worked to make him harder still. Hayden stiffened his spine, fighting the stab of piercing pleasure as every nerve in his body simmered, ready to be ignited.

She licked, taking her time, sliding her cool tongue around his tight skin. "Lie down and stop fighting me. I'm going to suck the cum out of your cock."

He struggled to resist but her hand was curved around his shaft, gliding up and down, the icy heat swirling inside him.

"I need it." She paused. "You can either settle back and give it to me, or I'll shove you back and take it." Then she stroked him again, the coolness of her hand now so familiar on his skin. "I really do like you." Looking up at him with her green gaze, she added, "Much better than my last one."

The links of the chain rattled as Hayden lay back and stared at the rough wood timbers running across the ceiling. *My last one.* There had been another man, in this exact spot, being used this exact same way. And maybe another before him. "What happened to him? The last one?"

She paused, lifted her head. "Do you want to meet him?" She rolled his balls in her palm.

"He's here?" His reply came out as a groan.

Instead of answering, she took in all of him. His tip bumped the back of her throat. His hips jerked. The chain shifted and the collar cut into his skin. Pain radiated to his shoulders as she continued drawing him in and out of her mouth. When he bucked, thrusting himself deeper into her mouth, she pulled away.

"What you really want to know--if he's one of us." She caressed him with her cool fingertips. "The answer is yes. But not all my others wanted to be turned."

His dick twitched from the need for release but he managed to ignore it long enough to ask, "You give them a choice?"

"Of course. We all had the choice. It wouldn't be right to do something to someone against their will?

Right?" She laughed as she slid her hand down to the base of his shaft, squeezed. Her laughter stopped abruptly. "That's enough talking, Hayden. Shut up while I take what I need."

She took him into her mouth, swallowing him deeply. The tension in his groin increased, circled tighter, stole the air from his lungs. He bucked against her mouth, thrusting deeper into her throat. The metal ring around his neck cut the flow air, making him gasp, as the first waves of his dense pleasure rippled through him. The rings of pleasure were cruel, circling his cock, spiraling upward and out, seeping through his body in a mad rush. Mattie continued working to get what she needed while Hayden, lost in the spiteful bliss, braced himself for the evitable. The orgasm came in as black smog. Mattie continued to move her mouth over him, sucking more after each jerk of his cock. She pulled every drop from him, then she moved away, still swallowing his cum as she got to her feet. She swiped the back of her hand across her glistening lips and spoke as if none of that had just happened. "I suppose you want to see Rachelle."

Hayden, still waiting for his heart to settle, moved the chain off his shoulder and nodded.

There was a long beat of silence, then she looked away. "You aren't going to like what you see."

Hayden swallowed hard.

She got off the bed, went to the stove and kicked it. Sparks flared. She kicked it again. Sparks flashed higher behind the glass. "Also, you really need to start thinking bigger, " she said. "Try to see what you aren't even bothering to look at. You're a thinker. Think." She crossed to the dresser beside the bed. "I'll take you to her. But remember, I warned you." Wood squeaked as she wiggled open a drawer. After the soft rustle of objects, she went back to the bed. "We'll have to...have to—can you put your ankles together?" She grabbed one of his ankles and yanked it toward the other. "This isn't going to hurt."

The leather straps she bound his legs with were reddish-brown and about an inch thick. It was obvious by the efficient way her fingers worked the straps into knots that she had experience with tethering. Once the straps were secured, she tugged on the binds. "You'll be able to walk fine. They're only there to keep you from running."

He moved his legs, testing the limits of the binds. "Where would I run to?"

"You're crafty, Researcher." She ran her fingers down his neck. "You might think you could build a dog sled and take off through the woods."

"Where are we?"

"See? That's what I mean." She tapped her temple. "You're always thinking." Then she pushed herself off the bed, crossed the room to take a loop of keys from a hook. "Why don't you do us some good and start thinking something useful for a change." She unlocked the chain from the wall then hooked the padlock on one of the hooks embedded into the wall.

"You never did tell me what you found out in the library, before I interrupted you."

He stood, adjusted the chain so it hung down his back, and stepped alongside the bed. The tethers were manageable. "Interrupted? That's what you're calling it?"

She closed the door of the wood stove. "I don't remember you complaining."

If only he'd known.

But looking back, even if he had, he may have fucked her anyway.

No. Not maybe.

"Tell me," she said. "What did you find out?"

"You didn't read my article?"

She tugged on the bands wrapped around her breasts. "Of course I read it, but I don't want that shit Bob wants."

"Are you seriously asking?" He sat on the edge of the bed and pulled the cover over his thighs and cock. "You know because you're proof of it."

She hung the keys then wiggled the drawer, wood squeaking until it was closed. "Tell me anyway," she said, perching herself on the table and placing her feet on the seat of the chair.

He described the tracker he'd read about, Guy Belmont, and how the man followed the tribe into the woods and watched them train those freshly turned how to acquire servants to live off the sex. After she prompted him, he told her about the drawings, and the few details of the sex rituals. She asked for more. "That really is all of it," he said.

"No, that's not all."

He shrugged. She was probably right. "I don't have the book."

"You should have taken it because there's more." She hopped down, walked to the window, stared out into the blackness. "Belmont is still around."

Bob would be thrilled to know that, but Hayden had no intention of looking the guy up. The man would do nothing but make things more complicated and more unbearable. He got up and tugged on the chain. The metal rubbed against floor. "Can you get this off?"

She shook her head, her gaze still fixed on something outside. "I want to know—" A sharp rap on the door stopped her. She shoved Hayden back onto the bed then pulled the door open a few inches.

A voice came through the narrow opening. "It's time."

She braced one hand on the wall and leaned into the opening. "I told him we were coming."

"Just doing what I'm told, Mattie."

"We're coming, Oscar. Tell him that." She pushed the door closed. "Matthew wants to meet you."

"I want to see Rachelle."

"You will." She went to the closet, pulled out a fur cloak, threw it at him. "Put that on." She ran looked him over. "Unless you'd rather go naked. Which I'm totally okay with."

Hayden threw the cloak over his shoulders, then lifted the chain over it. The softened hide caressed his skin as he covered his body. She wrapped a cloak around herself.

"Why bother?" he asked.

"Ice is bad for the skin after a while."

"No kidding?" he asked, sneering.

She stood by the open door. "Give me the end of the chain."

He held on to it. "You're not serious?"

"You want the others to know you're mine." She held out her hand. He handed her the last few links. His boots were by the door. She waited while he lifted the tethers and put them on.

They moved out into the night.

73

The snow wasn't as deep as it had been in the city, and the straps were long enough to allow him to walk in the footsteps she left behind. Running, though, would be a whole other matter. The cold too, would be a problem.

Tall pines sheltered the area, circling a clearing. Hayden spotted five more cabins. Two of them smaller, the other three about the same size at Mattie's. Hazy light came from each of the windows. A thin line of smoke came up from each chimney.

Tracks in the snow lead from one cabin to the next but other than that the snow was fresh. "You been here long?"

She cast him an indiscernible look over her shoulder.

"How many are here?" he asked, feeling the chill of snow clinging to the hair on his bare legs, creeping up his thighs.

"Count for yourself."

Cold crept up his calves, wrapped around his thighs. Was he counting those of the tribe or others like himself.

"Don't worry." She swung the chain. "They see you're mine, so they'll stay inside like good boys and girls."

"What about Rachelle?"

"What about her?" She took a long step forward, snapping the chain and jerking him along.

They left that clearing, stomped through a cluster of trees, came into a tighter cluster of tiny cabins. No candlelight in the windows. No gentle lines of smoke rising from chimneys.

"They're out. Getting what they need." The row

of tall pines ran behind all the cottages. The entire camp seemed to be circled by the enormous trees. The long branches heavy with snow, rays of the moonlight soaring through them. The setting was beautiful and the place appeared to be well cared for. It couldn't exist without anyone knowing. A scout camp? A retreat for businesses?

Might someone check on the cabins?

Not likely, considering the fierce weather.

The tethers occasionally caught in the snow, the chain swung, a weight on his neck, a constant threat to behave. They came to an opening between some bushes, a spot where someone had shoveled a wide, clear path. "One last thing," she said, pausing beneath the low branches. "I do all the talking. Matthew isn't nice, like me. Give him a reason, he'll make you sorry."

Hayden grabbed the chain, lifted it enough to relive the tug on his neck.

"Got it?" His actual agreement wasn't necessary. She turned back and ducked through the opening. He released the chain and followed. On the other side was a single cabin, long and, like the others, sheltered by snow-heaped the pines. This one was bigger, with two chimneys. Two rails of smoke rose, one from each chimney, pale-yellow light glowed from the windows. The snow surrounding the building was trampled in all directions. Two men stood at the door. A third sat on a grey pony, his legs swinging as his guided the animal toward them.

As they approached, the guards came forward. The one on the pony cast them a glance but swerved to move in the opposite direction. Mattie straight-armed Hayden. "Remember. Keep your mouth shut."

75

He grunted his agreement and she moved forward, offering a curt nod to the guards. They looked at the chain and Hayden did his best to tamp down the chill that ran down his back.

One of the two men on foot had a shaved head. He pointed to Hayden. "I want to see."

Mattie lifted the chain so it hung above Hayden's shoulder. "Open you cloak."

Hayden opened his mouth, ready to protest but Mattie cut him off. "Shut the fuck up and open your cloak."

The other man on foot had come forward and was also staring. "Price of admission pet."

Hayden complied, holding the sides of the fur wide enough for the men while he glared at them both. The bald one grunted. The other just leered. Mattie stood beside his shoulder, her shoulder turned away. The wind chilled his bare skin but it didn't come close to distracting him from the humiliation of having the men stare at his dick. Eventually, Mattie moved between him and the guards. "That's enough."

Hayden dropped the cloak.

She turned around, said, "Fuck you both," then lowered the chain and tugged.

Hayden tightened the belt as he followed Mattie across the threshold.

Square lanterns sitting atop low tables lit the interior. A row of five wooden chairs hung from hooks on the wall, and a stack of crates stood in the corner.

"This way." Mattie tugged on the chain.

They crossed the room and moved into a hallway. Mattie waited for him to catch up, then together they sliced through a set of hanging black beads. Side by side they walked down the hall until they reached a heavy canvas tarp. Mattie held the tarp aside and, still holding the chain, placed her hand on the small of Hayden's back and shoved him forward.

The room was large, big enough to accommodate a solid-looking bed piled high with pillows and blankets and a sitting area. The stove in the corner was larger than Mattie's, the heat more intense. A cabinet hung on the wall near a gold velvet wing-backed chair where a man sat, his legs splayed, his erect cock in his hands. A low table covered with an array of tin mugs and jars of herbs was beside the chair. Lanterns hung from the high ceiling, one on each side of him, casting shadows.

The man was lean and pale, with a shaved head and a row of earrings outlining one ear. An outline of stubble shadowed his jaw and cheeks. His chest was bare, light-brown leather pants shoved halfway down his thighs. Leather ties dangled below his balls. The man continued stroking his dick, his inked biceps and lean forearms flexing as he glided his fingers up and down. He was staring into a large wooden cage, across from him.

Locked inside, beyond the wooden slats, lay Rachelle.

Hayden moved as far forward as the chain would allow, then strained against it, feeling the metal cut into his neck. He kept pulling.

"She's a fine piece of ass."

Hayden twisted to look at the man, wincing when the neck ring cut into his flesh.

"Mattie made me promise to wait, and I have, but as you can see…" The man nodded down, "The wait is getting difficult." He palmed his tip, squeezed, dropped his head back, closed his eyes and moaned.

"Like you don't have enough to satisfy you?" Mattie gestured to the window, looked out into the black night. "You could have had Oscar bring you someone else. Anyone else. Why her?"

The man opened his dark eyes, rolled his head to the side and looked at Mattie through half-closed lids. "Have you dealt with the problem?"

"I will. After." She looked down, took a step back.

Wind howled. A branch cracked and hit the roof. Hayden felt the thump of his heart and the rustle of the hide against his skin. He tensed, watching the man.

"Hayden, this place is awesome. Check it out." Rachelle got up and paced along the rails, running her fingertips across them as she moved. She paused in the corner near him. Wearing a fur cloak like the one Mattie had given him, she pulled on the wooden slats, twisting and jerking. The cloak fell open, exposing her bare breasts until she hugged herself, pulling the cloak around her.

"I'm Matthew's captive," she said, her voice husky, playful. She turned, focusing her attention on Hayden. "I've been naughty. Matthew put me in here so I can be punished."

Mattie let go of the chain. It fell to the wooden floor with a soft thud. She moved further away from Matthew, her movements stiff.

Rachelle raised her hands and turned around. The cloak was split up the back to reveal most of her ass. She arched her back and grabbed the waistband of her blue thong as she wiggled her hips. "I'm a bad, bad girl, Hayden." She tugged the waistband down, using the panties to frame the bottom of cheeks. "What are you going to do about it?" Laughing, she pulled the underwear back into place, then spun, her mouth a circle of wickedness.

"I think she likes it here, Hayden. I hope you don't plan on ruining her fun." Matthew started rubbing his dick again. "I sure as hell hope you aren't planning on ruining mine."

Chapter Six

"But remember, I warned you."

"Matthew said he might lock you in here with me." Rachelle spread the cloak, letting it fall below her breasts. Her round curves were framed by the light brown fur, reminding him of the night before. But there was no expensive black lace lingerie. Not hint of intimacy. There sure as hell was no romance. "Maybe you can teach me not to be a bad girl." A shrill giggle came from her throat as she pulled the cloak back over her shoulders whirled, exposing her ass cheeks.

Hayden's nostrils filled with the smoke of burning wood and he felt the now familiar tingle in the back of his mouth as the iron-like scent settled into his mouth. He tried to swallow it away but it clung like moss then he scanned the room, searching as though the answer to what any of this meant might appear. Mattie's face stayed dull, her gaze not meeting his.

Matthew stuffed his dick in his pants, rose from the chair and then stretched his arms overhead. Skulls and barbed wire encircled the tree inked into one of his arms. The other was covered with tattoos too. The man groaned, put his hands on his hips, then, tipping his head at Rachelle, offered Hayden a slow feral smile. "Like what you see?"

His stomach rolled from lust, fear and disgust. He clung to the idea that Rachelle was playing some sort of game, biding time until they could find a way out of there. But that hope faltered when Rachelle crawled across the straw, laughing and wiggling as the cloak slid off. "Do you, Hayden? See something you like?"

Mattie moved over to lift one side of Hayden's cloak, exposing his hard cock. She came around behind him, untied the belt and let the cloak drop to the floor where it pooled at his feet. He stepped out of the heap of skin and fur, going toward the cage. The end of the chain rattled across the floor, then settled in a cold line down his spine when he stopped and put his palms on the slats. The expectation that he go into the cage hung in the air, and he breathed it in, savoring the sexual pull of what awaited him. Hayden considered fighting his own desire, but dark lust had seeped in, filling his lungs and blood.

Matthew unlocked the cage. Lantern light flickered across a long tattoo that ran down the center of his back, snaking from the base of his skull all the way to his ass. Before Hayden could make out the pattern, Matthew spun, pulling the door open as he stepped back. Hayden went in, the chain trailing. The lock clicked behind him.

Rachelle's skin looked warm and soft. Alive. She wiggled her hips and looked at him over his shoulder. But her gaze was cloudy.

Hayden eyed Matthew, who was again sitting in the wide, velvet chair.

"Yes, it's the same tea Mattie made for you. Just stronger. With an extra little something." Matthew looked at Mattie, still standing a few feet from the cage door, then to Rachelle. "She likes it, don't you, baby?"

"Oh yeah, mmmmm, but it's making me be a bad girl, Hayden." She dropped to the floor, writhing on her hands and knees, her muscular body a canvas of shadows. "You need to teach me a lesson."

He reeled back as his stomach quivered.

"What's the matter, Hayden?" Matthew taunted. "You losing your hard-on? You need me to come in there and help you?"

Rachelle crawled to the edge off the straw lining the floor and pushed herself back up to her feet. She tiptoed to Hayden, then took his cock in her hands, turning her head to the side. "I'll take care of him, Matthew."

But the other man was already on his feet, coming toward the cage. He wrapped his fingers around the slats and leaned closer. The scent of his body pressed in, a mixture of leather, cold earth and even colder sex.

Hayden spoke over the bile in his throat. "Did you already fuck her?"

"Actually, no. I was asked not to." He tipped his head toward Mattie. "You owe her for that."

"Common decency isn't enough of a reason not to?"

Matthew threw his head back and howled. His shoulders shook, his mouth open wide from the sound until he snapped it shut tipped his head toward Mattie. "We left that behind years ago. Best decision we ever made."

Hayden caught the wince Mattie tried to hide.

Matthew spotted it anyway and scowled. "Not now, Mattie. Not when we have this… entertainment."

Mattie crossed to the wing-backed chair, dropped into it, and stared straight ahead.

"Why are you just standing there?" Matthew asked Hayden. He lifted one dark eyebrow. "Take your boots off. Entertain me." He waved to Mattie. "Us. Entertain us."

Again, Hayden searched the room, looked at the doorway. If he simply ran out? What then?

Rachelle purred. "This is what I've been wanting. Something wild."

Hayden shoved her back onto the bed of straw. She fell willingly, spreading her legs as she tumbled. Hayden spun, tilted his head and offered Matthew a slanted smile of his own. "Let me guess. If you don't like what you see, you're going to come in here and show me up. Right?"

"Mattie told me you were different. Now I see what she meant." Matthew nodded, looking Hayden up and down. "I like fast learners, Hayden, but I don't think that's the only reason Mattie has a thing for you." His gaze darkened. "I intend to figure out what it is that has her so worked up."

"It's just the sex, Matthew," Mattie cut in, leaning forward but not standing. "Wait until you see him fuck her, then you'll understand."

"You sure it's just that?" he asked, still eyeing Hayden. "There isn't any more?"

"Look at him," she replied. "A tabloid writer. What else could there be?"

Matthew took his time, looking Hayden up and down. The other man's gaze was thorough, lingering, caressing. "You switched back to the metal neck ring," he said. A slow smile opened his teeth. He spoke

83

again, this time to Hayden. "Did she tell you why she put the ring on you?"

Hayden shrugged. "Maybe I don't care."

Matthew ran his palms down the wood slats. "You care."

Rachelle was beginning to whine and paw at his ankles and calf, but Hayden lifted his leg and shook her off. "If I care so much why don't you go ahead and tell me."

Matthew reached between the wood slats, grabbed the ring, and yanked Hayden forward. "She used to tie hers down with rope because she thought it was nicer, but the last one grabbed a log from the fire and set the bed on fire. We figured he was trying to burn the rope. To get away." The edge of the ring cut into Hayden's neck as Matthew lifted. "But maybe he was actually trying to kill himself because he hated Mattie so much."

Mattie had moved over to stand beside Matthew. "It wasn't the last one who set the fire. It was the one before him."

"Oh. That's right," Matthew replied, still holding Hayden, staring at him with harsh curiosity. "Right. Andre is still with us. Sort of."

Hayden inched closer to the bars to release some of the tension of Matthew's grip. "I could still burn the bed."

"Yes. But the metal ring she locks the chain to is bolted to a pipe that runs through the headboard and into the ground. So, yes, you could burn the bed, but it wouldn't give you a chance of getting away."

Rachelle got up and rubbed herself against Hayden. She'd taken the cloak off, and it was spread across the floor. "What are you guys talking about? You're boring me." She wrapped her arms around Hayden and tugged.

Matthew tightened his grip on the collar and pulled upward, making it cut into Hayden's skin again. The bleakness of the other's man eyes was deep and unmoving. The only emotion churning inside him was ugly resentment, so strong it radiated off his pallid skin. Not even the man's own unique icy scent was more desolate. "Make all the little comments you want, Hayden." He jerked the ring and pulled him close enough for Hayden to feel the chill of his breath when he spoke. "Mattie has some special interest in you. That means *I* have a special interest in you." He let out a growl, then suddenly released the ring. Hayden went back, tumbling across Rachelle as they both fell. "Now be a good boy and fuck your girlfriend for me." He scoffed as he glanced sideways. "I mean us."

Rachelle writhed beneath him, her body liquid, arms and legs sliding. The musky scent of her aroused body drifted up, mingling with the straw and smoky air. He rolled over, wrapped his arms around her and hauled her up into a sitting position. Kneeling in front of her, he brushed tangled hair from her face.

Matthew had settled into the velvet chair, his legs splayed, his erect cock once again in his hands, a fine gleam with an undeniable edge in his eyes.

Hayden caressed Rachelle's stomach, moving his hands upward. He felt the fullness of her breasts and the slow seduction of her breathing. The warmth of her body. Knowing what was expected of him made it easier to justify his arousal.

"What is it you like about this, Rachelle?" He

cupped her breast, and found himself waiting to squeeze it. Hard. But he held back. "What do you want?"

"Don't you get it, Hayden? The answer is the same for both questions." She slid one of her hands inside her blue thong and cupped her pussy, leaned back and ran her tongue across her lips. "Isn't it what you wanted? Isn't it why you came here?"

Hayden braced himself by setting his palms on the ground as he shook his head. "We came here because—"

"You're here now, Hayden," Mattie cut in. "And you know better than to sit there talking when you should be doing something more creative. More entertaining. Because right now you're boring all of us."

"Mattie." Matthew's voice was a low growl. "Come." He gestured to the floor. "Sit."

Mattie went, dropping down to sit cross-legged at his feet. Matthew combed Hayden's body with his gaze and he felt the stare sliding over his muscles, gliding across his skin, taking in each inch of bare flesh until finally saying, "Continue."

Every chance he'd had to say no he'd said yes instead. There was no going back now. Fear rolled across Hayden's shoulders, crawled down his back, and churned under the weight of the metal chain. He'd done this to himself. To Rachelle.

Guilty blood flowed through him, his human heart pumping the menacing liquid through his traitorous veins, stiffening his cock and readying his body for sex. Sliced of memories of the night before flickered in his mind and his blood thickened more, making his shaft full and rigid. It felt so good. Powerful. Dreadful. Rachelle took one of his hands and put it on her breast, her eyes glazed from the tea. "We're the show, Hayden."

She shimmied, forcing her breast into his palm as she pulled her other hand from her thong to grab the base of his shaft, wrapping her warm, wet fingers around his cock and tugging him forward. Still on his knees, he kept moving, the chain hanging from his neck, the leather bindings on his legs snaking behind him in the straw.

"Come closer, Hayden, put your dick in my mouth."

A jagged shiver ran down his back, vibrating off the chain. He had a sense of what waited for him if he chose the righteous path. If he refused to perform. But what about Rachelle? He'd dragged her into this. She was playing along, but she had no idea it wasn't a game. What would happen to her if he refused?

What was going to happen when he complied.

He rose up fully on his knees and then inched forward. Rachelle bent down, parting her lips as she crept toward him. She licked the underside of his cock as he slid into her warm, wet mouth. She moved her tongue over the underside of his shaft, gradually taking in most all of him. Hayden took the top of Rachelle's head in his hand, curling his fist, watching the strands of her dark hair tangle between his fingers. His blood heated, firing his nerves and he tightened his hold on her hair and used the grip to control the pace and depth of the thrusts. Behind him, Mattie's lifeless breath quickened. Matthew laughed lightly and muttered something Hayden couldn't hear.

His thrusts got wilder as lustful darkness swallowed him, dragging him back into a bleak sexual abyss. Hayden fucked her mouth harder, the need for release stole his breath and the last of his consciousness. Darkness swallowed him whole, decency replaced by deviance. He didn't care. Rachelle kept his shaft in his mouth, still sucking even after his last pulse of cum. With the end of his dick still in her mouth, she tipped her head and looked up at him from beneath her lashes. She grabbed his ass and pulled her mouth free. His cock was still slightly stiff, filled with the dark blood of evil lust.

"Lie down," she said, her lips glistening.

His hands were still in her hair, but sanity was beginning to return. He pulled on the tangled curls, bringing her closer. "You don't have to do this."

Rachelle grabbed the chain and jumped up, yanking the links, forcing him to his feet. "You're forgetting about me, Hayden. I need to be fucked. I need to be punished because I've been a bad, bad girl." She took a step back, yanked again. "That's why I'm locked in this cage."

Hayden searched her eyes for a sliver of the woman he'd left behind in Boston, the woman he thought he'd known.

"It seems you aren't up to the task, Hayden." Matthew shifted forward, the thud of his boots on the planks rhythmic.

Rachelle writhed as she licked her lips. "Come on Hayden, you--"

Two men pushed through the tarp, came into the room and stood, arms folded across their chests. Rachelle let go of the chain and it fell onto Hayden, smacking against this ass with a sharp snap. She stepped to the slats and leaned into then, shoving her breasts between the wood bars. "Hiya. Have you come to watch the show? The naughty show?"

Hayden wrapped the chain around his waist, tucking the end through. The links pressed into his hipbones, but it would be harder for anyone to use it to jerk him around.

Both men were wearing capes, the fur hanging low, ending just above the tops of their boots. They weren't the same men who'd been on guard out front.

Matthew turned. "Speak."

The man in front tipped his head toward the cage. "Maybe we should step outside?"

Matthew tugged on the laces of his pants. "This better be important because, in case you assholes didn't figure it out, we're in the middle of something."

One of the man stared at Rachelle's breasts before replying. "We have information." He cleared his throat and tugged on the red ponytail hanging halfway down his back. "I think we need to hurry up. Leave sooner."

Matthew snatched a coat hanging on a hook behind his chair. "Did I tell you to think?"

He shoved his arms through the sleeves. The other two stepped back to allow him to pass, then followed him out. The rumble of their feet faded into silence so complete the rustle of the pines boughs on the other side of the window sounded in the room. The wind howled and snow pelted the glass.

"He doesn't know why you're here," Mattie said to Hayden. "If you're smart about it, you'll keep it that way."

"I don't know why I'm here either," he said.

Mattie got up, strutted toward him. "You're here because I want you here."

Hayden pulled Rachelle away from the bars, shoved her to the side. "There's more to it than that, and we both know it." Rachelle stumbled back then leaned into him, wiggling, rubbing her ass across against his crotch. His cock stirred. He kept his focus on Mattie. "What is it you don't want me to tell him?"

She said nothing, just stared at him with her swirling, dark eyes.

"What?" he asked again, pushing Rachelle off his cock.

Mattie glanced over her shoulder, leaned in, a whisper on her lips. "You—"

Yelling came from the other room, high-pitched voices that carried down the hall. Mattie turned to stare at the doorway. More noise came from outside, shouts that cut through the night. Then, as quickly as it started, it stopped and she turned back toward the cage.

Shivering, Rachelle snaked her trembling her arms around Hayden. Her eyes had cleared, her smile more natural. He pulled her to him.

Mattie went to the cabinet next to the chair and clicked open a door. "More tea, Rachelle?" It wasn't really a question.

Rachelle pulled away from him and went to the slats, purring as she pushed her breasts between the slats again. The round swells being pressed by the wood should have been painful but she seemed to like the sensation. Mattie filled a mug, then stood before Rachelle, pressing the lip of the mug against one of her peaked nipples. Rachelle giggled and the sound made Hayden's stomach churn. After Rachelle giggled again, Mattie passed the mug between the bars. "Be a good girl. Drink it all."

Rachelle held the mug under her chin, emotions gliding across her face so quickly each blended into the other. "What about Hayden, he wants some too."

Mattie lifted her eyebrow. Hayden, looking at the red marks on the sides of Rachelle's breasts, shook his head.

Mattie filled another mug anyway, carrying it over to hold for Hayden. "Rachelle's right. You do want some." She slid it between the bars, held it out. "Drink it."

Hayden took the cup and pressed it to his lips. His body reacted to the smell, and he salivated, felt the pressure of blood stirring ion his veins. Lowering the mug, he nodded toward the doorway. The beads had finally stopped swinging and the silence surrounding them felt unnatural and threatening. "Who are they? What's going on?"

"Why do you care?" Mattie replied as she watched Rachelle gulp the tea.

"Tell me what's going on, and I'll let you hold Rachelle down while I fuck her."

Rachelle dropped her cup on the floor outside the cage. It tipped and rolled across the floor, leaving a thin trail of liquid that gleamed in the candlelight.

"I don't need your permission. Not for that, not for anything." Mattie replied, rolling her shoulders and making her breasts jiggle beneath the red bands. The blood in his veins quickened, his cock stirred.

"It'll be better if you do," he said. Then he thought of a new angle, so he added, "Rachelle will like it better if you have my permission." He reached for her, smacked her ass with his palm.

"That's right," Rachelle murmured, rolling her shoulders. "Hayden is the cage master."

Mattie pointed to Hayden's hands. "Drink it." A glimmer of green shone in her eyes. If he moved closer, her scent would fill his nostrils then sink lower and seep inside him.

Hayden tossed the mug through the slats. It hit the floor with a soft thud. Tea splashed and then dribbled as it rolled, stopping next to Rachelle's emptied mug. He reached down, stroked his cock. The smaller, subtler movement caught Mattie's attention, her gaze following the motions. He tipped his head toward the door. "Tell me who they are."

Mattie shrugged, not taking her gaze from his cock. "Watchmen. No big deal. We have lots of them."

Hayden wanted for more but she only stood, her green gaze fixed on his dick. "Unlock the door," he said." Come in."

Instead of doing as he said, she picked up one of the mugs, went to the cabinet and refilled it. She held it out for Rachelle. "Here, sweetie. This will keep you from hating your boyfriend."

"I could never hate Hayden. He's going to make sure I learn my lessons." Rachelle drank, then handed back the empty cup. A drop rolled down the right side of her chin. And she wiped it off with her index finger, then slid it into her mouth to suck the drop from her tip. Even after the liquid was gone, she continued sliding her finger in and out of her closed lips.

"Good girl." Mattie took the mug to the cabinet. "Now you won't remember any of this." She got the key, unlocked the cage door, then returned it to its hook. Inside the cage, she went straight to Rachelle, looking her up and down. The lazy smile fell from Rachelle's face as she backed up, her lip quivering as Mattie stalked toward her. "Where are you going, sweetie?" she asked her. "It's time to get fucked." She jerked the other girl forward, then threw her onto the straw. "How do you want it? On your hands and knees? Your back?"

Rachelle rolled into a sitting position, pulled her legs in and hugged her knees. "Why so shy all of a sudden? That second cup of tea hasn't kicked in yet?" Mattie put her foot under Rachelle's chin and lifted her face. "Hurry up and decide. I can decide for you if you want."

Fear moved over Rachelle's face. Her gaze slid to Hayden.

He shoved Mattie back. "I'm the Master. I decide."

"Really?" Mattie's eyes glowed brighter. "Then why isn't she down?"

"She'll be down when I tell her to be down. I have the dick. I'm the one who fucks her."

Mattie backed away from Rachelle and pressed her cheek to Hayden's. She ran her fingertips across the chain around his waist, then wrapped the loose end around his cock. Holding it, she whispered. Her breath crawled into Hayden's ear, her icy scent tightened the back of his throat. That smell…he was beginning to need it. Crave it. "I don't need a dick to fuck you—and your whole world. Remember that." She unwrapped the chain from his cock, then shoved him, but not hard enough to make him fall. Rachelle looked on, her chin on her knees, her eyes half closed.

After he regained his footing, Hayden leaned into Mattie, backing her to the bars, holding her there. He glanced down, took in the top of her breasts then leered. "What's going on outside?"

She turned, the tangle of her hair falling across

her face as she tried unsuccessfully to shove him back. "Don't start something you aren't going to finish."

He leaned harder, used his knee to hold one of her thighs to the bar. "Who says I'm not going to finish?"

"You don't understand what you're getting yourself into, Hayden."

Smirking, he kept holding, staring into her eyes. Behind them, Rachelle moaned softly, the sound reminding him of a muffled wail. Hayden held back a shiver and waited. The cabin was silent, the voices from outside had faded completely away. Only Rachelle's raspy breathing and the howl of the bitter wind remained.

Mattie stopped pushing back "Three of the dormants are gone. Matthew didn't pull them."

He slid one hand between them, worked it upward and tugged on of the first bindings he touched. Her cool skin shivered and he tugged again, exposing one nipple. Her breath hitched and her nipple tightened into a hard point. "What's a dormant?"

Mattie's gaze slid to Rachelle who had scooted back to the corner and was now watching them with totally glazed eyes. She turned back to Hayden. "After someone goes through the initiation, they stay dormant until the rites ritual."

Using his other hand, he grabbed the hem of her skirt and lifted. "More." He found her pussy and cupped it, applied pressure until she widened her stance. "Tell me."

He slid his middle finger between her pussy lips, felt the tight coolness, saw her chest rise from a sharp breath. "They're dormant. Not alive, not dead."

He caressed her clit and leaned closer to smell her cool skin. "And?"

"Obviously, they can't move. If they're gone, it means someone took them. It wasn't Matthew, so it had to be someone else. Not one of us. Shouldn't be, anyway. If it is one of us, we all have a big problem." She rocked her hips against his hand. "Whoever took them will be removed."

"Killed?"

She nodded. "Burned. Or cut up."

Hayden didn't care about their problems. "What is it you want with me?"

Mattie aligned herself with him, spread her legs, then moved her body again, getting the pressure where she wanted it. "Sex."

No way was he that stupid. "What else?"

She used one hand to hold the chain out of the way and the other to shove his hand out from between her legs. Then she grabbed his cock and wrapped her fingers around his hard shaft. Smiling, she guided it slowly inside her tight, cold cunt then rocked into him. Hayden drew back and thrust in. Mattie reached behind to grab the bars and hook one leg behind him, moving him closer, deeper into her body. He ground into her, barely pulling back before thrusting in again.

Mattie laughed. "By the way, don't worry about her. She won't remember anything. Not a single tiny thing."

Rachelle. He'd forgotten her and Mattie knew it, wanted him to understand his own betrayal. Angry, ugly guilt made him drive with a wild force that started to warp his consciousness. She matched his hard rhythm, using him as he used her. A strange grey haze fogged his mind and, weary and indignant, he gave himself over to it.

"What the fuck? This isn't what I want." Matthew

reached through the slats and grabbed a fistful of Mattie's hair, yanked her away from Hayden. He pulled again, she tumbled to the floor with a solid thud. A low green sheen appeared in the brightened the man's eyes.

Mattie righted herself, tugged her skirt over her pussy and yanked her red bindings up to cover her breasts. Scrambling onto all fours as she crawled out of Matthew's reach, she pulled herself up, slipped through the cage door. After she took her seat by the foot of Matthew's chair, she pushed her hair off her face. "What's going on?"

Matthew's finger flicked quickly as he unlaced his pants, released his cock. Even soft it was huge. "That's not your problem, is it?" he asked, caressing his cock.

"I have a right to know if we're safe." Not looking at him, she added, "And if there's someone around that shouldn't be trusted."

"We're safe here until I say so. Now shut the fuck up." The strokes of his hand quickened, his dick stretched. "Watch if you want, don't if you don't want. I don't give a shit, what you do, Mattie. Maybe you should remember that."

He stepped into the cage and threw off his fur coat. On all fours, Rachelle scrambled over, climbed on top of the coat. She rolled over and then started rubbing herself across it like a cat scratching its back in the dirt. She lifted her knees, then opened her legs, showing off her tight thighs and the pussy folds between her legs. "I'm glad you're back, Matthew," she said, eyes fully glazed as she grabbed her breasts then pinched her own nipples.

Matthew let go of his cock, but it was so tight it jutted forward, hard, ready. "Take the thong off, so we don't have to waste time tearing it off you." One side of his thin lips curled upward. "And spread out the coat. I hate that straw."

Rachelle peeled off her thong, then stuck her ass in the air, exposing the dark shadow between her thighs, as she arranged the fur beneath her. She lay on her back, arms stretched out overhead, her eyes unfocused. Matthew swung around and positioned himself above her, dropped onto his knees, then scooted forward until the underside his stiff shaft brushed her lips. She stuck out her tongue and licked his tip. Hayden took a step back. Rachelle licked again, using a long sweep to get the full length of the underside.

"That's right, little bitch. Lick it, love it. It's mine." Matthew used her hair to pull her head back then shoved his dick in her mouth, the green glimmer in his eyes nearly making his face glow. "Take more, take it all." He laughed, low in his throat as he forced himself in, making her gag.

Hayden's gut rolled and a chill of fear, heavier and colder than the wind outside, blew across his skin. He shivered, sucked in air and got a lungful of that smell. Bitter, infectious, and as powerful as it was unavoidable. The scent coated his tongue, settled across his molars and made him salivate deep in the back of his mouth.

Rachelle slid her feet to her ass, then dropped her legs open, exposing her more of her pussy. The slick curves of her nether lips glistened, her opening a welcome sheath. She was telling Hayden to fuck her, right there on the floor while Matthew shoved his dick in and out of her mouth. Hayden hated himself for wanting to. Needing to impale her. Jam his cock into her. Shatter her.

The nasty truth came from the back of his mind. If Rachelle hadn't insisted on following that damn map, they wouldn't have been there, stranded in the woods, captive. Lust, resentment, and self-hatred exploded inside him, then fought up from the black depths of his soul. He ground his teeth, trying to get the acrid taste from his mouth.

"Now you're getting the idea, Hayden." Matthew moved his hips back, pulling his cock out to dangle it above Rachelle's mouth. She licked his glistening shaft, her tongue looking small as she carefully stroked the underside as though tasting his dick was her ultimate pleasure.

Her pleasure, *her* decision.

That's what this was all about. What she'd wanted—following the map, coming here.

Rachelle reached up and took Matthew's cock in both hands, gently guiding it in to her mouth as she tipped her head back to get it deep in her throat until she had to struggle to take more.

Hayden's lip curled in disgust. For her. For himself.

"Something on your mind, Hayden?" Matthew asked, spreading his legs so his hips were closer to Rachelle's mouth. The man's gaze zeroed in on Hayden's rigid cock. "Because this isn't the time for talking."

Hayden was going to fuck Rachelle, and he was going to like it. He knew it. Matthew knew it.

"There's more where this came from, Hayden. I have enough for you, enough to keep you fucking all night. Women, men, whoever you want, however you want it."

"Fuck off."

Matthew's laughter made Hayden clench his jaw.

Once the howls subsided, Matthew forced his cock into Rachelle's mouth so deeply that his sac pressed against her temple. She choked then moved her head to get air. He rocked into her, jerking his hips back and forth, driving himself into her mouth. She continued gagging, her eyes wide, salvia running down from the corner of her mouth, but her mouth stayed open as though she welcomed the challenging punishment.

"Do whatever you want," he said. "She won't remember this, not any little second."

Hayden watched Matthew fuck his girlfriend's mouth, mesmerized by the rhythm of the man's body, swaying back and forth, rocking into her while she struggled. Each time he drew out, she gasped for air then sucked him back in, more spit streaming down the sides of her mouth and dripping onto the fur. Scorching curls of anger and disgust rose inside him, turning and twisting, silencing the last voices of his decency, giving space to the bleak fire of lust that flickered higher and higher.

Hayden stared down at Rachelle, his body stiff, tense and simmering with a low rage he hadn't known he possessed. The anger rose like steam, coming slowly then thickening, finding its own way, its own path. The sensation gurgled through him, filling his veins with new, wilder blood. Even the air he pulled into his lungs was different. "It's a well-crafted tea,"

Matthew said, taking his dick from Rachelle's mouth. She continued the licking motions for a few seconds, until her brain understood the cock was gone. "It dulls the mind just enough to quell the conscience shut down memory."

Rachelle lifted her chin and tried to connect her gaze with his, but the effects of the tea must have been too much because she gave up, turned away, began stroking her breasts then pinching her nipples as she rolled her hips in inviting circles. Hayden ground his teeth, let out a hot breath and looked upward. Unlike Rachelle's, Matthew's gaze was sharp. Brewing behind the awareness was an unquenchable evil that was as compelling as it was repulsive.

"If you ever wondered what she's really like," Matthew said, "you know, the person under whatever careful side she always shows you and everyone else, wonder no more. Here's the real girl under the mask."

Matthew jerked his hips, once again jamming his dick in and out of Rachelle's mouth. Each time she coughed, his mouth twisted into a snarling grin until she once again opened her mouth to rounded her lips around his shaft, diligently sucking, desperately working to give in to even the fiercest thrusts. "Good girl," he said, stroking the side of her head. "I know you'd die for me, to give me what I need."

"Watch this, Hayden," he said, shifting forward to put his cock into Rachelle's mouth, then holding it there. She struggled, a slick trail of saliva rolled down from the corner of her mouth as her eyes flickered shut. Matthew tilted her head back, adjusting better for several deep, belligerent thrusts. Hayden's own dick stiffened more, lifting until it jutted forward.

Hayden moved forward, feeling the weight of the chain on his hipbones and across his back as he knelt between Rachelle's legs. She showed none of the hungry urgency that had turned him on the night before. Now she was nothing more than a willing vessel for his lust, a place to shove his cock, a body to receive his pent up fury.

He unlooped the chain from his waist, let it hang from his neck to the ground.

"It's what's good for you, Hayden." Matthew paused. "Trust me, I know. Do it." Then he began again.

Hayden's own world hung on the fringes of his awareness, that place where right and wrong existed. He reeled back and soaked in the corruption, inhaled it in. Once the last of his consciousness faded into the wretched haze of his mind, he placed his cock at Rachelle's slick opening and impaled her. She bucked, the movement of her hips acknowledging his entry, inviting him to fuck her.

And he did.

He fell into the simmering fury, newly churning within him and drove into her. The chain swung beside him. He reached for it, but Matthew was quicker, snatching the end. It swayed above Rachelle, connecting them. Hayden threw himself back, trying to break the other man's grip on the chain. Again, the other man was ready, laughing with a tight grip. Hayden tried again anyway. The edge of the neck ring cut into his already deeply scratched flesh, a thin stream of blood ran down his chest. The red line hit the hair of his lower abdomen, snaking a path to where his body connected to Rachelle's.

Matthew held the chain taut, the swing of his hips

becoming sharper, wilder, his face a mask of sexual tension and fierce pleasure. There was no humanity in his eyes, only bottomless carnal hunger. Hayden joined him, pumping into Rachelle.

Her breasts bounced as he worked his dick into her, her whole body in motion. Hooks of darkness came to him and pulled him in, guiding him into the empty place of his soul where only he existed. He clung on the edge of awareness, then tumbled in. The fall was sweet torture, but even then he knew the scars would be with him forever. The rings of tension circled his shaft and gripped his sac, squeezing harder, tighter, pulling on the last threads of his humanity. A shiver ran down Hayden's back, igniting a ring of release that started at the base of his cock.

Across from him, Matthew's groans filled the air, the vibrations creating a raw wave of shivers that ran across Hayden's skin made his muscles knot and his teeth chatter. The rings of tension gripped him for long seconds, then began a slow, torturous release. Inch by inch, the circles widened, held then let go. The sensation crept across him, slowing time, taking pieces of his humanity.

After the last spasm of his ejaculation, Hayden dropped back onto his heels and swiped away the trail of blood on his torso. But that wouldn't erase what he'd done or how he'd felt doing it. Rachelle had faded into complete unconsciousness, her eyes closed and her entire body slack.

"Good work, Hayden. You fucked her out of her mind." Matthew, green glimmer gone from his eyes, tossed the chain down, then began caressing his softened cock as he got to his feet.

Matthew tugged the cloak out from under Rachelle, making her tumble across the straw. Her only response was a murmur. He wrapped it around himself, then braced his palms in the cage doorway. "Got to get going sooner than later, Mattie. Meeting in an hour. The lodge. Be there." He glanced at the floor then looked to Hayden. "Come alone." He leaned forward, stretched his back, the line of ink running down his spine twisting with the motion, then exited.

Rachelle's eyes were finally open but barely focusing.

Mattie had put on her cloak and was waiting by the door, hands by her sides, face blank.

The chain pulled on Hayden's neck ring, causing it to rub against the raw places where it had been cutting into his skin. He lifted the links to release some of the physical pain, but the shock of what he'd just done, been part of, lingered, settling into him, becoming part of him.

The first rays of the morning sun sliced through the window, illuminating the dust rising from the straw as Rachelle stirred. She moaned softly, then tucked her legs tightly to her chest and looked over her knees.

"I did what you wanted, Hayden. Brought you to your sweet Rachelle, so you could make sure she's all right. Being taken care of. Don't you want to thank me?"

Rachelle untucked herself, rolled onto her side, and tucked her hands under her cheek. "You wanted to come see me Hayden? That's so sweet."

Doubt and confusion he had expected, but shame and regret, those were two things he had not been expecting from his request to see his girlfriend. Disgust, another.

103

Mattie rapped on one of the slats of the cage. "Come. Get your cloak."

Hayden turned away from Rachelle, exited the cage, and handed the chain to Mattie. He put his boots on, then she led him from the room, back down the hall, through the room lit with square lanterns and out through the door. The two guards were still outside, one on each side, but the third on the pony was gone.

Streaks of morning sun sliced through the trees, making the snow heaped branches shine. Hayden stepped into Mattie's tracks, using her footprints to guide him through the snow. They walked between some shrubs but left on a different route than they'd come. After rounding a corner, Hayden spotted soft gray rings of smoke rising from a longhouse, the sort of building scout camps used for meals. He trudged on, his feet rising and falling in the snow, the faint scent of smoke surrounding him.

Low voices floated on the wind, but he couldn't tell what direction they were coming from. When he slowed to look around, the chain lifted then pinched his neck.

"What?" Mattie asked, holding the chain taut.

Hayden turned, listening for the sound but pretended to look at the yard. Soon he was studying it in earnest. Fresh tracks ran in every direction, circling the longhouse and an extremely wide-trunked tree. Probably a maple, judging by the arch of the branches and the overall shape. But it wasn't the type of tree he was most interested in, it was the trunk, scarred by a circle of tattered bark about three feet from the base.

"What are you looking at?" she asked, loosening the chain.

The circle of torn and broken bark was fresh. "Did you bring me this way to see if I'd notice the tree?"

Her mouth stayed shut.

He squinted against the sunlight reflecting off the fresh snow as he tipped his head toward the tree. "They do the rituals outside, even in the winter?"

Mattie pointed to the branches, some weighted with snow, others blown bare by the wind. "They think the tree adds power, vitality, to the ritual. The bigger the tree, the more energy it possesses. This tree gets a lot of use."

" *They?*" Hayden repeated the word, forcing her to recognize that she hadn't included herself with *them*.

She turned her back on him, spoke over her shoulder. "I could've brought you here last night instead of doing what you wanted, taking you to Rachelle."

"This isn't about what I want. It hasn't been ever since the start."

She shrugged, then shoved aside the edge of her cloak, exposing her pale thigh. A stream of melted snow ran down the inside of her leg and rolled down the curve of her calf. The trail of moisture disappeared into her boot, and he looked up, connecting with her gaze. She lifted an eyebrow. The memory of her perched on the library table and him shoving his cock into her tight pussy exploded in his mind.

Had he really wanted that? Really?

Her gaze moved from the tree to the longhouse. "Not everything's about sex."

Hayden laughed, a rough, dry bark. "Tell that to Matthew."

She winced, stepped back, and tugged the chain.

He jogged forward to release the sharp tension. "What's going on with you two?"

"It wasn't always like this." She lowered her hand, giving the chain some slack. "Things changed. He changed."

Overhead, a hawk screeched, cutting through the spiral of smoke rising from the chimney. Another swooped down to snatch something from a shady patch beneath a narrow pine. A third dove low, calling as it neared the ground but swept back up, claws empty.

They'd been standing long enough that the chill was beginning to make Hayden shiver. He tugged the cloak around himself. "What about Rachelle?"

Mattie scoffed. "What about her?"

Hayden gazed into the sky, watching for another bird as he repeated her question to himself. No answer came to mind.

"I want to go." Mattie turned, stepping through the snow with a long stride, soon quickening her pace, speeding up to a jog as she pulled him across the snow, toward her cabin.

Chapter Seven
"Don't try to play me."

The fire had burned down and the cabin was cold.

After locking the chain to the ring embedded in the bed, Mattie crossed to the cabinet beside the wood stove. Her shoulders jerked as she pulled out two cans of corned beef hash and set them on the table. She set the teakettle on the corner of the stove then stood with her back to him, arms crossed across her chest. "Since you didn't reply I'm going to ask again. Are you satisfied Rachelle is okay?"

Hayden kicked off his boots and, still wearing the cloak, pulled the bed cover over himself. "That's not why we went over there," he said, stiffening his muscles to ward off a round of shivers.

She spun on her heels so sharply she had to grab the edge of the table to keep from falling. The telling green gaze glimmered in her eyes. "You see, Hayden, that's why I need you. You're smart. You *think*."

"Fine, I get it. I think. What is it you want me to think about? It's not Rachelle. It's sure as hell not Matthew, either."

Still holding the edge of the table, she laughed, the sound sharp and humorless. "So far, so good."

She swayed, the green glimmer lingering in the

depths of her gaze. Sex she could get from any man, but there was something else she believed only he could deliver.

"How often do you need it?" he asked, sitting up and leaning back on both hands. The bed cover fell, the fur cloak, opened and dropped away from his shoulders. He ignored the chill in the air and held still as emerald gaze swept over his chest then lowered to the shadow between his legs.

"It varies." She leaned back heavily on the table and continued staring at him, the morning sun coming in from the window behind her streaking across her shoulders and the tangles of her hair. "We don't have any way to regulate. It can be hours, minutes, sometimes days."

For a fleeting second he wondered what she'd been like before. He brushed the idea aside. "Come here, I'll take care of you," Hayden said, so ready to find a way to take advantage of her weakness.

She disregarded him and started moving around the cabin, getting ready to start a fire in the wood stove. He watched her in silence, knowing sooner or later she'd take what she needed. Still ignoring him, she opened the cans of hash, put the contents into a pot and set it on the stove. Flames had started flicker behind the glass, and Hayden's stomach growled at the thought of hot food. After stirring the hash, she put a bucket near him, told him he could use it when he needed, then stacked more blankets on the other side of the bed. She went back to the stove to rearrange the wood. Her movements were automatic, practiced, like a hotel housekeeper arranging a room the in same way, no matter the guest. He was one of many. If he didn't figure out what else she wanted from him specifically he'd be dead or *around somewhere.*

The room had continued to brighten with morning light and the temperature was rising as flames ate up the wood. Weariness started to get the better of Hayden, his eyes grew heavy and he weary, he welcomed the temporary release of sleep. He lay back and started to pull the cloak over him, but Mattie stopped him as she climbed onto the bed and straddled him. That familiar metallic taste moved across his tongue,

She grabbed his dick and began stroking, gripping lightly, her hand moving slowly, carefully, gradually making his cock hard enough. "After I fuck you, you need to eat. You can reach the stove with the chain on. Then sleep."

Hayden closed his eyes.

"Don't try to play me, Hayden. I don't care if you enjoy it or not," she said, stroking him tenderly, putting more pressure on his shaft.

He turned his head, feeling the damp fur of the cloak on his cheek as she opened one eye. She was staring at his cock, her green gaze hungry.

Still fondling him, she continued speaking, the rhythm of her words matching the motion of her hand. "I could have made you drink the tea."

He nodded, remembering the cup he'd thrown, the second one Rachelle had so willingly drunk and Matthew's words. *If you ever wondered what she's really like, wonder no more, here's the real girl under the mask.*

Mattie caught him looking at her. She stared back, the sheen in her gaze bright. Her lips curled as she glared down at him and positioned herself above him. Once she had the opening between her legs directly above his dick, she said, "Don't make the mistake of thinking I like you." Then she dropped down on him, covering his cock with her cool, tight pussy, and fucked him.

* * *

Hayden knew he was dreaming and struggled to wake but the dream held him, gripping him in its sinister arms.

He was back by the maple tree outside the longhouse, but it was a late summer evening and the air was warm, humid and filled with earthy sweetness. Instead of icy and dotted by the last snowflakes of a blizzard, the night was the kind a person could stay outside until morning, cradled by the lingering heat of the day, reliving the vitality of nature's potency. In front of Hayden was a fire, logs stacked upright like a teepee. Flames roared, skipping up into the black air, embers floating toward the stars. Three women were tossing branches into the center of the upright triangle, the sweat coated muscles of their arms flexing.

The fire, like the night, was perfect.

The yellow and orange flames lit up dozens of faces. Seated in the grass, Hayden was part of a circle. Actually, there were two circles. One made of people standing. The inner circle, the one he was part of, was made of people seated cross-legged in the grass. Because of the fire in the center, he couldn't see all the way around but he could see enough to know the people seated were young, old, male, female, attractive, and plain. There was nothing about them that was similar. Except that they were alive.

Those in the outer circle were not. Each of them held the end of a chain, a rope, or a leash. Mattie was behind Hayden, holding the end of his chain.

There was no music and only very little talking. The most distinct sound was that of the fire, roaring as it grew. Tension snapped from person to person and most of those seated were still, eyes glazed.

Hayden turned and looked back over his shoulder. "Where's Rachelle?"

"She's there." Mattie jerked her chin up, indicating a spot several yards away. "Can't you see her?"

Hayden leaned forward, feeling the heat of the fire on his face as he searched the crowd. Mattie pointed to a cluster, but Hayden still didn't see her.

She kicked him. "No, not down. Look up."

Hayden wiped a bead of sweat from his cheek as he lifted his chin. Rachelle stood beside a black-haired woman about twice her age. The woman held a brown clay jug and two large brown mugs.

A thin line of dread worked up Hayden's spine as he watched the other woman fill the cups and hand one to a man at the end of her leash and one to the man at the end of Rachelle's. Obediently, the men drank, handed the cups back. Rachelle patted the top of her servant's head. He lowered his shoulders and looked down, letting her stroke him. Hayden took his gaze away from Rachelle and her pet.

Mattie leaned down and whispered into Hayden's ear. "She's not the girl you think she is."

One of the women who'd been tossing branches into the fire came forward. She strolled through the shadows, moving around the center, stroking some of the pets as she passed. She stripped off her clothes as she walked, tossing each piece to the ground, leaving a trail. Twisting and turning, she reached back to run her fingers over the tattoo along the base of her spine. Her skin glistened with sweat, her muscles were tight. As she moved, she cupped her breasts and looked upward.

She neared Hayden, and he recoiled. She dropped her hands, knelt in front of him, and reached for his arms. He leaned back, hit Mattie's thighs with his head. The woman shoved her tits in his face. Struggling for consciousness and finally woke.

* * *

Judging by the slant of the sun, it was late afternoon. He had to assume it was the same day because the fire was still going, low but enough to keep the frost out of the air. The pot of corned beef hash sat on the floor next to the bed. It smelled oily and sour, but he reached for it and the plastic spoon beside it. She'd also left a mug with what smelled like water, but he left that alone.

Even cold and congealed, the hash went down quickly. Lingering visions of the dream did not.

The images were vivid, even crisper than his recollections of the night before.

The heavy swing of the door made him jump. Mattie rushed in, then stopped short, staring at him. "What?"

Hayden ran his hand over his face, trying to wipe the fear and disgust from his expression. He lowered his hand and looked at her, feeling as if he was seeing her for the first time.

"You finally figured it out?" She crossed the room and sat on the table.

He put the pot on the floor, tossed the spoon in to it. "How does the initiation happen?"

She started swinging her feet. "It starts with a tea, one stronger than the one you drank in the car on the way here. Even stronger than the one we gave Rachelle."

Mattie went on to explain the initiation process. A person drinks the tea. The herb mixture slows their heart until the tribe leader—Matthew for them—has sex with the initiate. Climax and death must occur simultaneously.

"Some people die?"

Mattie hopped off the table, grabbed some logs from the stack piled by the wall and put them in to the stove. After shutting the door, she scooted onto the table again.

"Matthew usually strangles them, so yeah, some people die. That's the chance they take."

Hayden looked out the window, tried to guess how long he'd been asleep. "It's the chance you took."

She nodded.

Three o'clock? He figured. Not later than five, because the sun was still up. "You let him strangle you?"

"It wasn't Matthew who turned me, but yes, I was strangled. It heightens the orgasm." She tapped her fingers across her knee then worked the tips up her thigh. "But I bet you already knew that."

He ignored the jib and waited for her to continue.

"At death, they're a dormant. Stored until the tribe leader wants to revive them."

Hayden lifted an eyebrow, waited again.

She moved her hands to her knees, leaned forward and started swinging her legs again. "The revival is a simple matter of another elixir delivered into the skin."

"The spine tattoos."

Mattie nodded. "See, you are smart."

If it could be done intentionally, that revealed a new possibility. "How is it undone?"

"You see, Hayden?" She smacked her boots together. "We both want the same thing.'

"I have no idea what you're after." He let his sarcasm crack in his voice. "I want a better job and to pay off my student loans."

She smirked, the corner of one side of her mouth disappeared beneath her hair. "What do you need to do that?"

"*Information.*"

"Yep."

"You want me to figure out how to cure your tribe?"

"You're getting warmer." She stopped swinging her feet. "Except for one thing. Everything you find out is for my ears only."

"What makes you think I'm going to find out anything? And if I do that I'll give it to you?"

"That editor guy, Bob, he's creaming for more. He's one reason." She hopped off the table and collected the empty pot and plastic spoon. "I'm the other. You go get me what I want, and I'll leave you alone."

"You'll let me walk?"

She nodded and put the pot on the table.

Why were they pretending he had a choice? If he didn't do what she wanted, he'd be right back where he was, chained to her bed or worse.

"Why can't you go find it yourself?" She glared at him, telling him she wasn't going to answer. "Rachelle? What about her?"

"She'll be free to go."

"Just like that?"

"Just like that. You understand what's at stake now and what can happen if you don't deliver. So you'll deliver."

"Why should I trust you?"

"You don't have to trust me." She came over to stand beside the bed. "You just have to do what I tell you to so that I don't fuck your life up and leave your girlfriend locked in that cage."

He tapped the metal ring around his neck. "Who's going to service you while I'm off getting this *information*?"

"Thanks for your concern but it's unnecessary."

He watched her from the corner of his eyes.

She smirked as she held out her hand. "I realize that for you to do what I want, I have to let you go. It isn't like I can follow you around like some kind of stalker." She laughed, a tight, harsh sound. "Well, I could, but I don't have to in order to get what I want. Do we have a deal?"

No choice really. He accepted her hand and shook.

Chapter Eight

"She's not the girl you think she is."

The next morning, Hayden trudged through the clumps of gritty, brown snow covering the sidewalk, clutching his phone to his ear, wincing at Bob Keeler's shrieks of joy. For once the two of them wanted the same thing and as usual Hayden had a plan for how to get it. It was possible that within 24 hours he'd have delivered what Mattie demanded, given something to Bob that would make him even more giddy, and he'd be rid of the whole sick mess.

"Excellent. More, more, more." The man barked. "I want it all."

He wasn't going to get that. Not even close. But he'd get enough.

Wind whipped around the corner of the library building, biting Hayden's skin, reigniting the new chill that now lingered inside him, tingling just below the surface of his skin. Hayden tucked his scarf into his coat and buried his chin into the knot at his throat, bracing himself for the last steps to the library. Bob, barreling on, didn't even notice that Hayden wasn't responding beyond a half-hearted mumble. Even though he had slept in his own bed the night before and things seemed to be somewhat under control, he was not in shape to deal with his aggressively enthusiastic boss.

"I'll make the call for the convention pass, and double check on Belmont, that fucking weirdo author, make sure he's going to be there. Asshole better be. I've sent the man a few emails--copied you on some-- but so far he hasn't gotten back with me. You know how those writers are--arrogant. Evasive. Total pains in the ass. You pin him down. Talk to him. Get details. Get something good."

Hayden knew what he meant. He'd seen the emails. It hadn't been *a few*. It had been dozens.

Bob rambled on about what he expected to happen at the convention, so he murmured another agreement and clutched the phone to his ear. Hayden's concern for Rachelle, delivered to her own apartment just before Mattie had left him at his, still lingered. The assurance that his girlfriend just needed to sleep it off didn't sit well with him. What sort of long-term damage had been done? Wouldn't she notice the physical after effects of that *session*? Was she going to wake up, find herself bruised and sore and then come looking for him? He had no reasonable explanation for what'd happened. The best he could hope for was to get what he needed from Belmont and be rid of Mattie.

The sarcasm in the man's voice sparked some life into Hayden, and he finally managed to speak a complete, coherent sentence. "Right, I understand what you want." Good thing his boss never wanted any actual proof that what he printed he was true, because no way in hell was Hayden going to provide that.

After another round of coughing, Bob barked a curt goodbye. Hayden dropped his phone into his pocket and then rounded the corner. The entrance to the library was about a half block away. It would've been easy, just ducking inside and getting what he was after, except Mattie stood on the steps, her tangled hair hanging across the shoulders of her leather jacket as she turned to face him.

Doing his best to return her brutal stare, he kept going forward, stopping in front of her and taking in the slices of pale flesh visible between the binding straps. Without trying, he remembered how her big tits felt, pressed against him or filling his hands. Stop looking, he told himself. "Thought you weren't going to stalk me."

She laughed, her face looking oddly human in the bright afternoon sunlight. "Stalk you? Isn't that a little extreme?"

That quick glimpse of her skin, the memories of it, were enough to make his body respond to her. He did his best to ignore it, but his blood had already started to thrum, his heartbeat slow and heavy. Sex. That's all it was, yes. But not on his terms. Was it ever going to stop? The need. The want. The fear. "I understand now, nothing is too extreme."

Mattie's lips twisted as she dropped onto one of the low, snow-covered steps of the library. She crossed her legs, dangling one booted foot above the icy clumps dotting the concrete then looked around, her gaze moving slowly through the surroundings, assessing threats measuring possibilities. There was neither. The streets were humming with cars, shuttle vans and delivery trucks, but the sidewalks were mostly empty, so even though her reply was soft, he heard her easily. "I lied."

He propped one foot beside her and leaned down, close enough to see the tiny bits of ice clinging to feathery ends of her lashes. That was a mistake. Instantly, he sensed the vapor of tension that constantly circled her, spiraling around like a vortex of motion. If he let it, it would pull him in again. "What're you doing here?"

"What do you think?" She uncrossed her legs and set her palms in the snow beside her, and angled forward, close enough for him to smell her skin and feel the icy chill surrounding her. "I don't trust you," she said.

The images he'd been trying to squelch all morning tumbled through his mind, taunting him, reminding him of what he'd been part of. What he'd done. No matter how he justified it, he knew part of him had craved it, wanted to do it. He didn't trust himself around her either, but still forced himself to not back down. Keeping his nose near her cheek, he asked, "So you're going to follow me around?"

"Nope." She leaned back, swung one leg over the other. Hayden caught a glimpse of her bare pussy. "You go ahead. I'll be here. Waiting." Her sneer told him she'd flashed him intentionally and was satisfied by the way he'd taken the bait.

Why bother hiding it? Why give her more satisfaction? He made a point of looking over her pale legs visible beneath the fishnets and below the tiny skirt. Her torso was hardly covered by the red strips of wool. If that wasn't enough to get her noticed, she also had on the black leather jacket. "You don't think you're going to attract some attention, sitting in the snow in a miniskirt?"

"What the fuck do you care?" When he kept staring, she made a show of zipping up her jacket then squinted against the sunshine. "In case you haven't figured it out, Hayden, I'm not the kind of person who can walk into the library unnoticed. At least out here, I can disappear if I need to. That isn't a possibility in there."

Even though that was true, he'd rather have her with him so he could keep track of her. Until she was cut out of his life for good, apparently he had to find a way to deal with her random chaos. "Anybody lifts an eyebrow at you, you can tell them you're part of the comic convention."

She scanned the area, then shook her head. "No thanks, pretending to be someone I'm not isn't my thing anymore. Just get that book, bring it to me."

Maybe it was his imagination, but he was beginning to think she seemed anxious. Jumpy. "Everything okay?"

"Again-what the fuck do you care?" She closed her legs and tightened herself in a ball. "Go get the shit."

Thinking about Bob, he said, "We're going to look at it together."

"I may be a liar but I'm not the sort to back out on my word. A deal is a deal."

Delivering the book was the first piece of their agreement, the easy part. It was the second part—the unknown—that worried him. He had no control over what that book did or didn't tell them. "I'll be back in a bit."

"I know you will." She turned, looking away, pretending to be watching the traffic but her attention was not focused on the cars and trucks.

He backed away, leaving her there in the middle of the snow and ice to go inside.

A longhaired guy was perched on a stool behind the counter. Hayden nodded at him as he rushed past and headed straight for the stack where he'd found the book.

It wasn't there. He looked around, checking the shelves above and below, in case the book had been put away in the wrong place. The one he was after, by Belmont, and the two others that had been next to it were gone too.

Shit.

Fuck.

What sane, normal person would suddenly want those books?

No, not sane. Not normal.

Hayden bolted from the stack and headed to Bates Hall. It wasn't totally empty, the way it had been on that night. A few college students hunched over books and tapped on laptops. A single girl was already asleep, her long red hair hanging over her arms. He took another look around. That guard had to be around somewhere. Hayden crossed the room, weaving between the tables, the vaulted ceiling making his footsteps echo. The historic beauty of it all was completely wasted on him as he passed through the Government Information room, cut through the Abbey Room.

He was just reaching the stairs to the third floor when he saw the blur of the blue security uniform right as the man ducked into the Boylston Room. Hayden called after the guy and after a pause, the man turned around.

"Remember me?" he asked, moving forward. "I was here the other night, you know, when we had the storm?"

The guard twisted his too-full lips, as he looked Hayden up and down. "Yeah, man, I remember you. Zombie guy."

Something was definitely wrong with the guy, but Hayden hung tight and persisted. "Right. That's me."

"You left that book on the table, open. The lady that works the front desk in the morning found it— God knows what she was doing up here—and she came after me, telling everyone I left it there, just because I was talking about the zombies. You know, warning people to be ready and all." The guy squinted and leaned closer. Close enough so the scent of stale coffee blew across Hayden's face. "She's one of those older ladies, you know the kind who thinks she has the right to tell everyone what to think. Anyway, she waved that book around and made a fucking stink about those pictures. Told everyone I was some kind of pervert."

"Sorry about that." Hayden faked an apologetic smile and tried to be patient.

"It sucked pretty bad." The guard squinted again, leaned even closer, and jabbed one of his chubby fingers at Hayden's chest. This time he was so close that he could see a gold crown on his top back molar as the guard added, "Really bad."

Hayden softened the fake smile into what he hoped look like sympathy. "I bet it did."

The guy suddenly seemed to rethink his situation, leaned back and folded his arms across his chest. "You come here again to look for it?"

Hayden nodded.

A tall, sinewy older man with a long grey ponytail who was strolling past paused to great the two of them with a curious hello. "Something going on here in the library?" he asked, lifting his eyebrows. The man lingered longer than was polite or even normal. The guard's face soured even more and he waved the guy away, but the old man didn't move on. Instead, he squared up in front of Hayden, a speculative tilt to his head, and stared at him.

The guard cleared his throat. The old man stayed put.

Why did the library have to be so full of weirdos? This guy had to be someone he'd met at one of the off the wall cultural events he covered, he held out his hand. "I'm sorry, Sir." Hayden held out his hand. "Do I know you?"

The man didn't even blink. He just stared. "Not really."

Hayden couldn't care less about whether he knew him or not. He simply wanted to remember if the guy was someone important. Judging from his odd looks and lack of manners, he could easily be a fellow journalist. But there was something different, something drifting up from the back of his mind telling him to be careful and not in a way that would protect his career. He opened his mouth, opening some intelligent response would come to mind, but didn't have the chance to say anything because the guard shoved the man aside. "Need to keep this area clear, Mister. Safety reasons." Then, in what the guard no doubt hoped was an authoritative tone, added, "For safety and security reasons."

The man cast the guard an icy stare that made Hayden take a step back, but he moved on without another word.

The guard wasted no time in catching Hayden's attention by coming forward and again poking him in the chest. "I thought you'd be back. Seeing as you left in such a hurry."

Hayden glanced at the fat fingers lingering under his chin but decided to keep up the fake friendly repertoire instead of smacking the guy away. "You were right. I went to look for the book on the shelf, but it—"

"Wasn't there." The guard dropped his hand and started circling Hayden.

Hayden tried to widen the fake smile. "You know where it is?"

The guy kept walking. "Yep."

"Could you get it for me?" he asked, clinging to the patience.

"The way I see it, you owe me." He came to a stop behind Hayden.

Hayden dropped the smile and looked over his shoulder, wondering again about the old man. The guard wasn't looking around, he was staring straight at Hayden with his dull eyes. "I really am sorry about that lady. I'm sure that sucked."

"It did." The guy leaned in, to add, "You know what else sucked?"

Hayden's stomach knotted. "What's that?"

"Looking at those pictures of you fucking that hot girl. Pictures, when I could've seen it up close and personal if I'd been in the right place at the right time." He frowned. "How was I supposed to know you were gonna fuck her? I know those shots on the *Weekly*'s site didn't do her justice." The guy lifted his hands and spread his fingers. "That girl had some big, juicy tits."

Hayden dropped the smile and changed his approach. "Did you stop to think you might be talking about my girlfriend?"

The guy dropped his hands as he laughed, the appalling scent of endless cups of cheap coffee filling the air. "That girl ain't nobody's girlfriend. Even I can see that."

"What about the book? Can you get it for me?"

The guard took out his flashlight, started flipping it through the air and started walking again. Each time the metal landed in the guy's palm it made a fleshy smacking sound. "You're forgetting what I said." He paused, flipped the light twice, then said, "You owe me."

"You took the others too, didn't you? The ones that were shelved next to it."

"I sure did. I know you smart types always come back. And I was right." Two more flips of the light, then, "Here you are. Hope you're ready to pay up to get what you need."

Hayden looked for his wallet.

The other man slipped the light back into its holster then grabbed Hayden's arm. His thick fingers curled around Hayden's wrist. "No, not like that."

"What?"

"I want what I missed." He tightened his grip. "The girl. In person."

Hayden yanked his arm back.

"I can't do her, 'cause I have a girl myself. But I can watch, that's not cheating."

"You want to watch me fuck that girl?"

"Yep."

"You're serious?"

The man had the nerve to look insulted. "What's it to you? You used her to sell papers."

A mistake that never ended. "If I go get her now, and we do it, you'll give me all the books?"

"Now?" The guard used his fat fingers to smooth his hair then straighten his blue uniform shirt. Then he rose up on tiptoe to look over the shelves. "She's with you?"

Hayden headed toward the stairs. "I can go get her."

"Meet me in Rabb Lecture Hall in seven minutes. It's in the basement." The man pulled out his phone and checked the screen. "Don't make me wait."

* * *

He burst outside, squinting into the sunlight. No matter what he had to do, this nightmare was going to end. One way or another, this nightmare was going to end.

Mattie was right where she'd put herself, squatting on the step, scanning the traffic and surrounding area. She was so focused on watching, he got all the way up to her before she noticed he was there.

"Come on." He grabbed the collar of her leather jacket and hauled her onto her feet. "It's your turn to perform."

She yanked back, pulling herself away from him. "What the fuck is wrong with you?"

He reached again, grabbing the collar of the

jacket, and dragging her up several steps. "We're going inside."

"I don't want to go in there," she said, digging her feet into the snow then slipping on a patch of ice by the door. Once she found her footing she shoved him. He grabbed her hand and pulled hard, whispered into her ear. "You want the book? You have to go in."

Once they were inside, on the stairs headed to the bottom floor, he gave her a brief explanation of the deal he'd made.

"Whatever, Hayden. Nothing surprises me anymore." She shrugged out of her jacket and thrust her shoulders back. Her nipples were stiff points beneath the red wool. "It's not like I haven't done this sort of thing before."

They reached the basement, found the right door, went in. A stage was on the left and raised, stadium-style seating filled the area on the right. The only light in the large auditorium was a spotlight focused on the center of the stage.

The security guard's voice cut through the darkness. "On the stage. In the light."

Mattie swung up onto the stage and went straight to the spotlight. She stood there, dangling her leather coat in one hand, lifting the hem of her skirt with the other. Light streamed across her, illuminating her skin, brightening her face.

Hayden climbed onto the stage, turning to stare out into the darkness then forcing himself to move to the center. All he had to do was fuck Mattie more time. So what if that asshole was out there, watching in the darkness? One quick screw and he'd get what she wanted and what he needed.

When she reached the bright white spot in the center, Mattie dropped the jacket and lifted the hem of her skirt higher, exposing the highest curve of her cold, muscular thighs. She moved slowly, lifting the edge without the urgency he'd come to associate with her and sex. There was no green glimmer in her gaze. Instead, her eyes were a steady brown, framed by long lashes he'd never noticed before. Her hair, its usual mass of tangles, outlined her shadowed face

He paused, suddenly unsure as he saw her in a new way. She'd once been more than walking sex, a creature with unavoidable tits and the kind of long legs a man fantasized about having hooked around him. She hadn't always been the kind of woman who made a man feel right in all the wrong ways. Yet she'd made a choice to leave that behind and so now he too had a choice to make. "Hey fuckwad," he yelled into the blank space of darkness. "Do you have the books? With you?"

"I'm not an asshole."

Gritting his teeth, he grabbed the end of his belt, jerked it free. "Do you have them? Yes or no?"

The guard's irritated snarl was followed three solid smacks, cracks that sounded like he was hitting the books against the back of a seat. "That's all of three of them. Hurry up and hit that sexy bitch before I light this shit on fire."

Hayden let his pants drop to his knees.

"You aren't hard," Mattie reached for his cock.

He meant to push her hand away and take care of it himself, but he found himself watching her hand wrap around his shaft, slowly curing her fingers around his soft dick. Her palm was cold, but his body succumbed to her touch. He braced for the fierce carnal hunger, but it didn't wash over him or even trickle down his spine.

"Put your hands on her tits."

Mattie paused, her fingers stilled, and she arched her back, sticking her breasts out. He reached. The strips of wool were dry, and one by one, he tugged the bindings down, freeing one breast then the other. The weight of her heavy flesh filled his palms. She leaned forward, and he flicked his thumbs across her tight nipples. She closed her eyes, dropping her head back to reveal the soft skin of her neck. The ratty chunks of her hair swayed across her shoulders. A clump of ice fell and created a rivulet than ran downward. After a murmur, she lifted one leg and secured it around his waist.

She reached around him to grab her foot, then rocked, using the tip of his shaft to caress her clit, and said, "Let's get this over with." But instead of guiding his dick into her pussy, she continued to sway, rocking back and forth, using the gradual motion to get constant friction on her nub.

He went along with what she wanted, swaying, feeling her cool body get wetter and wetter. Gently, her reached around and cupped her ass. "I like it," he said, without thinking.

For a split second she stalled, tensed, then he felt a gradual change. It was almost imperceptible, but it was there, a flash of rigidity that turned into indifferent acceptance. "Fuck me, Hayden," she ground out, the words a command, then she guided his dick into her pussy, further and further, until his tip bounced against her wall. He raised his hand to curved one arm around her waist.

Still holding one breast, he drove into her, feeling the wet, cool tightness squeezing over his shaft. She bucked against him. He matched her rhythm, rocking into her, sliding in and out, feeling the inside of her body as though it was his first time with her. She groaned and held on to him, arching her back, moving her body with practiced perfection, pumping with increased speed and skill. He bent down and tried to suck her nipple but their bodies were moving too quickly so he began kissing her icy flesh instead.

The guard's voice slashed through the darkness. "Give me something to watch, asshole. Make it fucking hot."

Hayden froze, then moved back.

The voice came again. "You want the books? Start fucking like you mean it dude."

Mattie continued writhing, showing her body off for a creep she'd never ever see.

There was nothing to do now but get it done.

Hayden moved his hand around to her back then lifted her skirt, grabbed her ass with both hands. He pulled her closer, ground into her pubic bone, and waited for the bleak promise of dark sexual release. Instead, he fell into a different kind of abyss, an unfamiliar one filled with torrid lights and disturbing colors. Still he waited for the harsh, soul-blurring orgasm that always same with sex with Mattie, but instead found himself sharing her own sensations, felling her slick walls squeeze his cock as she came. Her quickened breath was soft against his neck, whispers of air that gave him a different sort of chill.

Their exchange was completely different, dishonest in ways he couldn't comprehend right then and knew he wouldn't want to think about later. Even before the last pulses of cum left his cock, Hayden shoved her away then jerked up his pants and hooked his belt.

Mattie avoided his gaze as she lowered her skirt and tugged up the red wool straps that barely covered her flushed breasts. "I'll meet you out front." She hopped off the stage and headed to the door, her boots striking the floor with a heavy thumps. Her jacket trailed behind her. A flash a light same from the hall when she passed through the door,

The guard was marching down the aisle, his wide middle swaying side to side as he moved. "It wasn't hot like before."

Hayden leapt off the stage. "Fuck you, asshole."

"No, fuck you."

Hayden lunged forward, grabbed the man's arm, twisting it behind his back as he wrenched it upward. "You got what you asked for. The books."

He guard grunted. "What if I don't?"

Hayden lifted the man's arm, shoving it up between his shoulder blades as he guided the guy further up toward where his voice had been coming from. "Start walking, I'm right behind you."

The guard should have known, even wonder kids had their limits.

* * *

About an hour later, clutching the straps of his backpack, Hayden rounded the corner then paused, looking at the white blink of the tiny lights hanging from the trees lining Commonwealth. Some of the

131

snow was gone from the branches, so the lights glowed more brightly than the last time he'd bothered to notice. It was all so lovely, so normal. But it was just that, an illusion.

"Very, very pretty." Mattie stood beside him, looking over the Instagram perfect scene, but the snarl curling the corners of her mouth assured him that she too felt out of place there.

Instead of replying, he started walking again, moving his gaze back to the grey sky and heavy clouds. They had the books, now he had to keep on and see what more he could find. Thanks to an all-access press pass Bob had arranged him for the comic convention starting the next morning, Hayden would be able to get to every event—including the cocktail party being put on by the publisher of that book. The author was going to be there, probably downing the custom drinks created around the party theme. Maybe the guy would drink enough alcohol to tell Hayden every little thing he knew. If the drinks didn't do the trick, Hayden would find another way to get the information. Any other way.

The thud of Mattie's boots sounded from behind him. They hadn't spoken since meeting up on the library steps. The only exchange was her grabbing his shoulder bag, digging through to make sure he had the books, then shoving him in the direction of his apartment. They'd be inside in a matter of minutes, finally getting a chance to read through the book. Hayden was doubtful the book was really going to deliver anything significant. Most likely, that information was going to have to come from the man himself.

Once he got more, Bob Keeler was going to be thrilled, out-of-his-mind ecstatic. It was almost time to get Bob to deliver on that promise. In a couple months, if he made it through this, Hayden might not be avoiding his student loan payment app or dodging those pain in the ass questions at parties. Shit, he'd like to see the looks on his cohorts' faces when his feature stories started showing up in *The Globe*. This stint at the *Weekly* would be a thing of the past, something to put in his bio to amp up his street cred.

A couple strolled the boulevard, swinging their arms as they walked. Four kids, bundled up so much they could barely move, circled a lumpy snowman. The hat they'd brought for him was an oversize straw sombrero embroidered with flowers, probably a souvenir from Mexico. Across from them, an old man sat on a bench, huddled into his coat and scratching his collie's snow sprinkled head. Back Bay Boston on a dark mid-December evening. Snowmaggeddon was a memory and, except for the piles of snow, the harsh blizzard forgotten.

Except for the impulsive, dangerous creature trailing behind him, just beyond his shoulder. He turned, ready to break the silence between them by asking her what she expected to find in the book, but she was gone. He stopped dead, dug into the shoulder bag. The book by Belmont was gone too.

Chapter Nine
"Start fucking like you mean it."

Friday about noon, Hayden shoved through the mass of gyrating bodies. The stink of nervous energy, stale sweat, and cheap rubber clung to him like a second skin, and every time he brushed against another of the convention attendees, the sheen coating his skin got thicker. The threat of another announced that morning had done nothing to slow the crowds. The place was wall-to-wall comic nerds, milling around in a collective trance. Everywhere he turned, there was another cluster--larpers carrying swords and wearing leather, women in tall white socks and short plaid skirts, but most of all there were blood-soaked, tattered and torn zombies. All of these freaks were hoping to catch of glimpse of their favorite artist, writer, gamer, or, thanks to that damn movie, zombie actor.

As for him--he was dressed in jeans and a green Pendleton sweater, and looking for that one man. The asshole who, now that he thought of it, was to blame for the whole fucked up mess. What kind of person tracks a tribe of zombies anyway? Then, considering his own actions, banished the query. Apparently, though, Belmont thought he was some sort of too famous to meet face-to-face rock star or a politician seeking immunity before talking to the press. One damn email, the man could've answered just one fucking message. Hayden had been at the convention for almost two hours and so far, nothing. The all-access pass wasn't doing him much good. Each reception room he'd been granted entrance into seemed to be packed with other low-level press hoping for any sort of scoop and other all-access pass holders, standing around, getting in the way.

Get done with this, he kept telling himself. Get done and get back to life. What was left of it. Like Rachelle. She hadn't been answering his calls or returning his messages. No surprise there, really. She had every right to be frightened or disgusted. Every hour, every minute, the images, intruded his thoughts. The memories were so dense with sensation they were more like impressions, thoughts embedded deep in his mind, buried behind his emotions.

The gut wrenching possibilities of what more might happen to Rachelle if he didn't get rid of Mattie plagued him. His own realities, the ways Mattie had used him for the past five days, the things she'd forced him to do, filled him with shame. It was his responsibility to get her away from them all. If only that was his only motivation for hunting down the man who'd written that shitty book that had started the whole shitstorm. He had a sense that he needed to get to him before Mattie did. There was no telling what she'd found in that book. The not knowing was killing him, but if he got to her first that wouldn't matter because he'd get the man to tell him what was in the book and more.

There is was…the ultimate humiliation.

He hadn't hated all of it. Worse still, he was beginning to crave it. The depravity. The freedom delivered by the inhumanity of it. It was wrong to want it. That release without consequence. Want her. Wanted more. Wanted to give her what she wanted, to truly satisfy her instead of just hold her off until the next time. He winced at the thought, knew how ugly and dangerous it was and began understood all too well why Guy Belmont had spent time in their shadows.

Hayden picked up his pace, rounded a corner and ran into a mob of high schoolers, faces downward at their phones, bundled into a tight cluster and blocking the way of everyone around them.

Fuck.

He made a sharp right, then stopped short when he literally collided with someone.

"Hey dude, watch where you're going."

Hayden came face to face with yet another zombie. Or, to be more accurate, someone's interpretation of a zombie. The guy's grey and brown make-up, torn clothes, and fake blood smeared into his dreadlocks looked nothing like *them*. The woman beside him had a similar thing going—a torn tan bodysuit and B movie horror makeup. She definitely didn't look anything like *her*.

"Sorry," Hayden offered after realizing he'd been staring. Waving his hand upward, he added, "Um, great make-up."

Bodies pressed in from all directions, nearly locking him in place.

The guy, also sandwiched between people, jerked his head up and down. The dreadlocks bounced against his shoulders. "Good enough to win, ya think?"

136

Hayden looked beyond their shoulders, scanning the crowd. "Sure."

"What about me?" the woman tapped him on the shoulder then shimmed when he looked back to her. "I'm trying for that so-scary-its-sexy look."

Hayden blinked. "Oh."

"Not enough?" The woman tugged on her body suit, pulling it down so more of her tits showed. "I'll show more of my boobs. I don't care."

The guy grabbed his crotch. "For that prize? I'd put that make-up on my cock, make it look like its rotting away from my balls, and walk out there naked."

Hayden continued searching the crowd, hoping to get an idea of where to look for that man next. A locals only press room? He could try calling Bob, see if he had an idea. But that meant talking to the man and Hayden was definitely trying to avoid that.

The woman managed to get herself in front of him, blocking his view and any possible exit. She pulled her zipper even lower and shook her breasts again, then asked Hayden, "How's this? Still not enough?" Then, to the wanna-be zombie guy, she said, "You should totally do that with your dick! We'd totally win."

Hayden's stomach knotted at the thought of seeing that guy's cock. "What's the prize?"

A pair of people in a unicorn costume came through the stew of bodies, knocking the zombie woman off balance and making her fall against him, tits first. Once she got her footing back, she replied with an awkward wink. "Drinks with that guy, the zombie dude."

Hayden extracted himself from her grip and got out of the way of the unicorn before it had a chance to run in to him. Maybe he could get Bob off his back by getting him interested in something else and buy him a little more time to get at Belmont. "You mean Rodney McKinnon?"

The noise from the swarm of people grew even louder and the guy had to yell over the low roar. "Nah—we don't care about those *Zombie Rites* actors. What a bunch of wanna-be *Walking Dead* stars."

The woman was readjusting the tops of her tits. "We're going to that contest for the writer. The one who wrote that sex zombie book."

The guy wrapped his arm around his not-nearly-sexy-enough woman. "You know, the researcher that wrote that weird ass sex book. You know, the one about the tribe."

An announcement from the exhibit hall speakers droned from above, announcing the start of the *Sex Tribe* contest in ten minutes. The woman jabbed her guy with her elbow and pointed upward, toward the sound, then started shoving through the crowd.

Hayden's words came out in a near squeak as he moved closer to them both. "Guy Belmont?" he started pushing through the bodies around him, trying to keep up with the couple as they moved away "What's the prize?"

"Drinks." She replied over her shoulder. "With him. Tonight."

"Best sex zombie costume, that's the contest. Two winners, man and woman." The guy pushed aside two of the high schoolers who'd stopped to take selfies with the unicorn, opening a path between the mob.

"You going there now?" Hayden swerved around the unicorn, caught up with them again and tapped the guy's shoulder. "To the contest?"

"Yep." He jerked his arm overhead. "Follow us. For the win."

The woman glanced back at Hayden, her grin an uncanny contrast to the deathly makeup covering her face. "You aren't planning on entering?" She lifted an eyebrow, looked him up and down as she bounced along, giggling. "Are you?" Her laughter grew louder as the zombie guy tugged her through the crowd, her head jerking back each time he tugged her forward.

Hayden shrugged in response.

Laugh all you want. You're not winning this contest.

He followed behind them, searching the crowd again but this time for Mattie. She was there-- somewhere. Among the people, lurking in a hall, or crawling in the rafters. He knew she was near because he felt her, even since arriving at the convention. Her iron-laden scent had begun to seep through his chest, into his lungs. Soon he'd smell it on his skin and feel it deep inside. Then it would flow through his veins, making his blood thick and his cock pulse.

From in front of him, the zombie couple left the main wing of exhibitors then turned into a hall that was less crowded. They moved more quickly and Hayden followed, still looking, watching. Waiting. She had to need him soon.

Right then he needed her too. But not for the sex, he told himself.

Maybe she found someone else and used him instead.

139

He should be relieved.

At the end of the hall, they ran in to a mob of zombies in every possible state of tattered dress to nearly naked undress. A raven-haired woman wearing a tight black T-shirt dress and red vinyl thigh-high boots was sorting the creatures into two rows, men and women. The couple he'd followed in had already split apart and placed themselves in the lines, one of each side of a stage. Most of the chairs for the audience were full, one row of spectators waved their arms to the techno music humming from the stage speakers. Hayden backed up, flattened himself against a wall. A sudden chill rippled across him and he pulled his coat tighter, shoving his hands into the pockets.

The line of women zombies snaked out in front of him, gyrating. Every body type was represented. Every type but hers.

"Have you been looking for me, Hayden?"

He didn't have to turn to know it was her, but he did anyway. She moved closer, brushed her leg against his and stared at him with her icy eyes.

"Get in that line." He looked away from her and pointed. "You have to win this contest."

"Since when do you tell me what to do?"

He reached for her, ready to shove her into the line, but she sidestepped, neatly avoiding his grasp. "This isn't the time. I'll explain later." He pointed to the woman so intent on exposing her breasts. "Get in that line."

She took a step forward, and Hayden noticed a man who'd been standing beside her. With his salt and pepper hair, basic beard, and average height he didn't look like one of her tribe, but he was watching them both with a peculiar interest, a bizarre gleam in his brown eyes. The man held out his sunspot-covered hand. "Hayden?"

Hayden slid his hand from his pocket, slowly, letting his fingers brush the palm of the other man gradually, fearing that familiar chill. But the man's hand was warm and his grip light.

"Um, yeah, I'm Hayden." He followed through with the rest of the handshake, but the man didn't let go.

Still gripping Hayden's hand, the man tipped his head toward the row of female zombies starting to climb the steps leading to the stage and nearly yelled over the now blaring techno. "I have you to thank for all this."

Hayden nodded vaguely, tugged, finally extracting his hand then pushing Mattie toward the stage. "Get in that line."

She spun, shoved him back, pinned him to the wall. His blood stirred when her breasts brushed him, the memory of their constant fucking so fresh and vivid it made his bones ache. "I know something you don't know, Hayden." She pressed in to him, jabbing his ribcage with her elbow. "As usual."

Hayden grabbed her arm, wrapping his fingers tightly around her forearm as he tried to yank her arm away. "Get in that line."

She eased back and sneered. "After I get in the line, what do you want me to do?"

The man pushed himself between the two of them. "Be yourself. Win my contest."

Her sneer shifted into an inelegant leer, directed at him. The man took two steps back, rolling his shoulders into his battered safari jacket. She slipped her fingertips under the red bindings wrapped around her chest. "Hear that Hayden? His contest."

What the fuck were they talking about. "Your contest?"

He unhooked his shoulders some and nodded. It took longer than it should have, but he figured it out. This little man in the ridiculous safari jacket was the very man he been looking for, the one who'd been ignoring him. "Belmont?"

The guy straightened his back even more. "Please. Call me Guy." The man smacked Haydn's bicep. "I feel like we're friends already."

Hayden bit back the *fuck you very much* for not answering any of Bob's emails. Who did this asshole think he was?

"You wait here. I have a contest to win." One side of her lip curled upward as she looked down at his fingers, still squeezing her pale flesh. "Why the stupid expression? You don't think I'll make the cut?" She moved her gaze to his face. "You worried about my feelings? That'll I'll try to cry on your shoulder?"

"If I were the judge, I'd pick you. That's for damn sure." The man made a point of staring hard at Mattie's tits, then pinched the hem of her skirt and lifted it to expose one of the holes in her fishnets. "And you know, I am the most credible judge."

Guy's grating laughter was so out of place it made Hayden's skin quiver and his nerve endings jump.

Still sneering, Mattie flicked Guy's hand away. "You're both so sweet." Then she slipped into the center of the line, ignoring the complaints coming from the women she'd cut in front of.

142

Hayden cut his eyes toward the man who was staring hard at Mattie, pushing her way to the front. A few minutes later, she was on the stage, rolling her hips in rhythm to the music. Bending, writhing, curling her foot behind her while her arms arched up reaching for a pole that wasn't here. Disgusting. Sinister. Beautiful. The music continued. Hayden had to watch. Knowing that the old man beside him was also captivated repulsed him, but not enough to keep him from looking away.

One by one the other women backed away, their lips twitching with fake smiles, their shoulders hunching as they ran into each other, forming a cluster at the edge of the stage. A few of the men were still moving, doing what they could to keep up with her but even they were intimidated. None was her equal and they all knew it.

"I'll give you all my notes for a night with her."

Long seconds passed. When he said nothing, the man repeated his request, his stale breath rasping into his ear. Hayden finally pulled his gaze away from the stage, slid closer to Belmont and looked at him, really looked at him. The man returned the scrutiny, unflinching. "You don't know what you're asking." He shook his head, the small and slight. "You really have no idea."

The man lifted his chin as he gazed over Hayden's shoulder. "Tell me what you see?"

He didn't need to look. She lived in his imagination now. He gestured to the stage with his thumb. "The w--"

"No." Guy tapped on his own chest. "When you look at me."

143

Hayden took a step forward, putting his back to the stage and blocking Guy's view as he gave him a careful once over. A short, weak-looking old man with grey hair and a L.L. Bean travel vest. Beige khakis and sturdy boots. Nothing much, that's what he saw.

Guy lowered his hand rolled his head as though loosening his shoulders. "You don't need to protect me."

Protect him? That'd been the last thing on his mind.

Behind them, over the crushing music, the crowd began to howl. The air vibrated and the sharp, escalating tension in their collective voices filled Hayden's gut with trepidation. If only they knew. Understood.

He leaned down, images of the cage, the tea, and that night with Matthew swirling through his mind. "You don't understand what you're asking for."

"Do you want the notes? Don't bother answering because I know you do." He unzipped the highest of the pockets covering the front of his jacket, took out a black thumb drive and held it up. "And I have the rest, original drawings and all, in my hotel room."

The howling continued, building more, apprehension tightening the air. Maybe that anxiety didn't belong to the crowd. It belonged to him. He stared at the man, an old loser who'd gone to college long before student loans became the unbearable burden of everyone over the age of 25. "Why are you asking if you already know?"

"Don't forget the emails and that Facebook message. You boss is a little bit desperate I'd say. That makes you desperate. Right? I'm glad for the reaching out though. Gave me plenty of time to think about what I wanted in return. Now you know. One night with her."

Hayden eyed the flash drive. It looked like a dollar sign and represented freedom. "I don't own her. She does what she wants."

Guy held it up, inspecting it as though it was a precious gemstone. "That's not what she told me. She said I had to get your permission."

"And I'm telling you, you don't need my permission." The ear-piercing howling continued, blending with the music. The people who'd been staring nearby had moved to the stage, so now the space around them was clear. "She's going to win. She'll be your prize."

"All that means is that I don't have to waste time with some fake zombie assholes." Guy slipped the thumb drive back into the pocket, zipped it closed, then patted the pocket. "Give me permission for my night, and I'll give you what you want."

The noise behind lowered suddenly. "Yeah. Fine. But you don't know--"

Guy's brown eyes took on a new sheen. "I tracked them, watched them, lived in their shadows. I know everything about them but I never got to...experience it. Them. The life." He moved away from the wall, leaned in and took a deep breath. "I know you have. I can smell her on you."

Hayden recoiled, then reminded himself he'd left behind doing the right thing and caring about other people was part of his past. Now he needed what he needed—information and a way out. For him. This old man could do whatever the hell he wanted. No matter how stupid.

Isabelle Drake

"I don't care what it costs." The man continued, sniffing, that gleam in his gaze getting thicker, filling with carnal darkness. "I know what I want and finally, after all these years, I'm going to get it."

It was only then that he remembered Rachelle. The thought followed quickly by a twinge of responsibility. Hayden wanted a way out for her too.

Chapter Ten

"You don't understand what you're asking for."

At exactly 10:30 that night, Hayden knocked on the door of Belmont's hotel room. After Mattie'd won the female half of the contest, the two of them left the convention center--with the thumb drive and the male contest winner. The old man had been alone with her and the other winner for hours. There was no telling what scene awaited him on the other side of the door. No matter, he wanted what he wanted and now was not the time to stop. He knocked again, louder and harder than the first time. This time, the noise was followed by muffled voices, a thump and then by a low laugh that made Hayden's gut constrict.

The door swung wide, hit the wall with a thump, then started to swing shut again, but Hayden grabbed the edge, eased it open and stepped through. Guy was retreating down the short hall, his pale, wrinkled flesh completely exposed except for his ass covered by his blue and white pinstriped boxers. Averting his gaze from the man's pathetic body, Hayden followed him to the end of hall. The room was a suite, with a sitting area, lighted balcony and modern kitchenette. The thermos was on the granite counter, one tin mug next to it.

"Hello Hayden." Mattie was perched on the back

of the couch, her feet, still in her boots, had made a wet patch on the floral cushion. Behind her, a slice of the Boston skyline glimmered, the lights blinking, a reminder of the normal world. The beige walls were accented with artistic black and white photographs of Boston's historic districts. Mattie's leather jacket was on the floor, beside the heaped pile of Guy's clothes. There was no sign of the male winner. Used and thrown away, no doubt.

"Hello Hayden." Mattie said again. Louder the second time as she leaned forward, put her palms on the inside of her thighs and spread her legs. "I have something you want and another thing you need."

The lighting in the room was too dim for him to see into the darkness under her skirt. He didn't need to, though. His body was already responding to her unspoken request and he moved toward her, everything else in his mind fading. Without thought, he reached for his belt and pulled it free from the buckle. The metallic jangle caught Belmont's attention, his pale face shifting quickly.

"We've been waiting for you, Hayden." The man came out the shadows, crossed the room, and stood beside the pile of his clothes.

Hayden let go of his belt, dropped his hands to his sides.

"I insisted we wait." She slid one hand further up her leg, working it up slowly, dragging it across her skin until it was far up enough to cup her pussy. "Guy's been impatient but you know me, I found ways to settle him down. Let him have some fun with our guest."

Hayden glanced at the mug on the counter.

She smirked. "He loved the tea almost as much as Rachelle."

Belmont didn't even have the decency too look uncomfortable, and Hayden wasn't about to ask for details.

"Stop looking like a sulky asshole. That loser loved it. Ten minutes ago, I put him in an Uber and sent him back to BC." She glanced at the floor. "Thanks to Guy, he'll have a few bruises and some scratches. He'll wake up tomorrow wishing he could remember what the hell happened to him." Pointing to the counter, she asked, "You want some? There's enough."

Hayden went to the counter and poured the remainder of the tea into the mug then crossed the room, held it out for Guy.

The man accepted it, wrapping both hands around the mug and lifting it so quickly some splashed over the edge. He drank the contents, set the mug down, then licked the sheen of liquid from the tops of his fingers. He slid his hand into his boxers. "Can I take them off now, Mattie?"

Mattie didn't look at him when she replied. "No. And you aren't ever going to take them off. Not for me, anyway." She stood on the couch, pivoted, then bent forward. "You can watch Hayden fuck me." She glanced over her shoulder, the fresh green in her eyes cutting through the dim light as she flipped up her skirt to expose the solid curves of her bare ass. Her thighs flexed, the muscles fluid beneath her white skin. She smacked her cheeks then dropped her skirt. "What are you waiting for?"

Hayden finished unbuckling his belt then unzipped his pants.

"This is supposed to be about me, my night. Why don't I get a turn?"

Hayden kicked Belmont in the ribs. "Shut the fuck up."

"What about what I want?" The man recoiled. His gaze shifted from Mattie's bare ass to Hayden's hard dick, now fully exposed. "This isn't fair."

Fair? No, none of this was fair. What did it matter anyway? Hayden sure as hell didn't. Mattie still needed him and as long as she needed him he had some power over her. He planned to use it.

Mattie had turned to face the window, and her reflection filled the window. The iridescent glow of her emerald gaze mixed in with the lights of the skyline, but the gleam didn't blend. He lifted her skirt and grabbed the waistband of her skirt. Then, he jerked her toward him and positioned himself behind her so he could push the tip of his cock between her ass cheeks. She wanted him to thrust in immediately, but he'd learned over the past few days that making her wait gave him a measure of satisfaction. The illusion that he had a choice about whether or not to fuck her.

He'd grown accustomed to the subtle iciness of her skin. Even the inner recess between her ass cheeks was cool. She arched her back, and he moved in, finding the tight opening of her pussy. Below, from his spot on the floor, Guy's breath grew loud and uneven. Hayden tried to ignore the noises as he thrust in but soon he felt the man's fingers wrap around his leg.

He lifted his leg, struck out and connected with Belmont's side without breaking rhythm.

Mattie laughed and bucked against him. "That's right Hayden, give Guy a show, make sure he sees what's he's not getting." She looked back over her shoulder to the man on the floor and sneered. "What he's never going to get."

The man whimpered.

Hayden's pumped harder, deeper, rougher. Willing his mind to go blank, telling himself not to enjoy her tight cunt squeezing his cock, he held on to the waistband of her skirt and pounded in. The lights of the city shifted in his gaze, the darkness of night swirled. He jerked his hips, squeezed his thighs together, made himself stiff. His orgasm came on suddenly, sharp as a dog bite, and ended just as quickly, leaving him feel bitten and ashamed. Again. Within seconds, Mattie was yanking her skirt from his hands. She leapt from the couch.

"Are you still waiting for a thank you?" She gestured toward Belmont. "Hayden? Stop looking at me that way or I'm going to ask you to jack him off."

Hayden looked up from zipping his pants. "Ask me?"

She reached down and grabbed the collar of Guy's vest heaped on the floor. "Up. Get off."

He rolled to his hands and knees then backed his palms to his feet to stand. He looked at Hayden with tea-glazed eyes. "You can do it if you want, you know."

"What?"

Guy had shoved his boxers down, taken his dick out, and had it resting in his open palm. "Jack me off."

Hayden averted his gaze as he hooked his belt.

Mattie tossed the jacket down. "Where is the thumb drive?"

"I didn't get all I wanted." Half-heartedly, he

started stroking his half-limp dick, his glazed eyes unfocused and his jaw loose.

"Thanks to that stupid contest, you got more than you deserved you twisted pervert." She wrapped her hands around his throat and shook him until he let go of his cock. "This is all a game to you, some kind of joke."

He grabbed at her fingers, trying to pry them from his throat. "I—you—"

"Where is the thumb drive?" She shook him harder and lifted him from his feet. "Listen up mother fucker. This isn't a game and I don't care one shit about you."

Finally, they were going to get what they'd come after.

Lifting him higher, she lowered her voice to an intimidating whisper. "You're going to give me that thumb drive—and the notes—right now."

Hayden tensed. The thumb drive, the notes, they had to be there somewhere. They had to actually exist.

The man hit the floor with a hard thud after she let go. "But—"

Her open-handed smack made his head snap to the side. Rubbing his face, he crawled across the room and pointed to a closed door. "Back of the toilet. Floating in a Ziploc."

"Fucking unoriginal place to hide shit."

Less than a minute later, she reemerged from the room, a piece of plastic sticking out from her leather pocket and a tattered brown journal in her hand. Weathered edges of paper stuck out from the journal. She stood at the end of the hallway, flipping through the papers. "This it? All of it?"

Belmont nodded.

She loitered a few seconds longer, the threat in her stare silencing any of Belmont's additional complaint.

Then she was gone, the slam of the hotel her last comment.

Chapter Eleven
"Are you still waiting for a thank you?"

"That backstabbing bitch." Belmont whined, still rubbing his face. "We had a deal."

The door to the adjoining bedroom was stood open, Hayden slipped through it. The bed was made, a closed backpack on top of the grey-striped cover. Both nightstands were clear. He cut across the room, into the bathroom. A row of brown prescription bottles lined the counter, a razor and bar of soap sat in the sink. Even knowing he would find nothing, he lifted the back off the toilet. Empty. When he turned to put the cover back on, he slipped. As his foot went out from under him, an empty plastic ice bag floated into the air. He reached for the shower curtain, grabbed a handful of the fabric, tore the curtain from the rings and landed in the tub.

He wasn't alone there. A body, wrapped in burlap, was beneath him. Only the head was visible. Grey skin, frosted eyes stared upward. Hayden scrambled, realized there was another body beneath the one he'd landed on. That one was also wrapped in burlap, secured with twine, the head exposed, with frosted eyes and cracked lips.

By the time Hayden was out of the tub, Belmont

stood in the doorway, his soft arms crossed over his sunken chest. The man was pouting.

"Those are mine."

The stolen dormants. Icy. Cold. Both alive and dead. "How did you get them?"

Why did he need to know? Mattie would want to know. Matthew would really want to know. He didn't really give a shit, but he was already considering the bargaining possibilities the bodies represented.

Belmont grabbed the curtain, he hands shaking as he covered the bodies. "Why should I tell you anything? You didn't help me. You don't care about us." Gently, he realigned the heads with the bodies then tucked the curtain around the bound limbs. "These special ones are mine." He looked at Hayden, his face soft. "Do you know what to do? How can I make them want me?"

The man lowered himself to the toilet and sat, then reached out to pet the stringy hair of the one on top. "Mine. My special ones."

Hayden put his hand on Belmont's crotch, moved it around until he found the man's soft cock. The pinstriped fabric was moist, disgusting, but he squeezed the man's shaft, gently trying to massage some life into it. Then asked, "Is there more tea?"

* * *

It was after two in the morning by the time Hayden had the second dormant secured in his own apartment bathtub. Eight sacks of ice from the 7-Eleven were packed along the sides, six more were crammed into his freezer. Unlike Belmont, he didn't want to see their ashen faces, and stare into their steely

155

eyes, so he'd yanked the burlap until it extended over the heads. Then he'd pulled the shower curtain closed and went to sit at the foot of his bed.

And wait.

It had started to snow again, the small flakes whipping past the window panes. A couple times he picked up his phone, thought about Rachelle. He couldn't blame her for not messaging back. After this last round was done, he'd go to her place. Explain? Probably not. Relieve his guilt? Maybe.

Around 4:00, the tapping on his window broke through his daze. She moved her fingertips across over the glass with a rhythmic, circular pattern, her face, blurred by the frosted glass, moved beyond. Icy clusters clung to her tangled hair, the weak light from the street made shadows on her neck. He stayed on the bed, waiting, staring into her green eyes.

She dug through the ice on the ledge, pried her fingertips beneath the bottom of the window and lifted. Gliding foot first through the window, carrying with her the whisper of cold from the night, she crept in. The chill, the night, it came in with her. And her scent, it came and reached him too. His jaw clenched, blood ran hot, skin tingled with the desire to give her what she'd come for. But only that.

She stepped toward him, her boots making a soft thump on the wood floors until she stopped in front of him. The snow melted, left two shimmering trails that widened and ran into the corners of his room. A new tear had opened up on the stocking on her left thigh. He slipped his index finger into the hole, tugged, watched the hole widen and the fishnets cut into her skin. With a quick yank, he made the hole even bigger.

Her leather jacket hit the floor after she rolled her shoulders back. "You're changing Hayden."

He thought of the bodies in his bathroom. "Are you?"

A snicker, then, "No."

"Do you want to?"

"No." She grabbed one of his ears and twisted, forcing him to lift his face to her. "Not in the way you mean. Understand?"

"What if you could?"

"You're not being very subtle." She touched his chin. "If you want to know what's on the thumb drive, just ask."

"What about that journal?" He slid his palm under one of the binds. "Did you look through it?"

She grabbed his ear and twisted it, sending spikes of pain up and down the side of his face. He understood her methods now, so didn't back off. He pulled his fingers from beneath the bindings and cupped her breast, then covered the nipple with his mouth. The point stiffened, and he sucked on it, flicking it with the tip of his tongue. The pain from his ear eased as she released some, but not all, of the pressure. Slowly, he pulled the peak further into his mouth, continued the caress. A bit more of the pressure of his face eased. He reached up, took her hand from his ear, lifted his mouth from the breast and slid her fingers between his lips. A few seconds passed, the two of them acting like lovers, until she grabbed him under the arms and threw him backwards, across the bed.

"You aren't the first one to try that." She straddled him, grabbed at the waistband of the sweats he'd put on when he'd first gotten home. "I'm not going to start caring about you, or fall for you, or some lame shit like that."

Beyond her silhouette, the snow flickered by the window, spots of white cutting through the night. The night, the snow, ice, it would always be a reminder of her. "Matthew? Did he try that?"

She yanked down his sweats, freeing his dick. He reached up, grabbed her shoulders and wrestled her over, pinned her leg with one knee. "Is that why you hate him?"

Staring up at him with her green eyes, she reached up, grabbed one of the bindings pulled it up, over her head. Shifting, she reached for another section and did the same, then continued the motion until the one long piece was on the floor. He'd not seen her without the red binding, and free from it she looked softer. Almost a woman. To think of her that way would be a mistake.

No more mistakes.

After lifting his knee, he said, "Tell me."

Rolling her shoulders in, her curled up and reached for his cock. "Pay attention to what matters."

He leaned back on his heels, keeping his dick in her hand, she rolled up toward him and slid her calves behind her. With light stokes, she skimmed her fingertips up and down the shaft. The chill of her touch sent shivers up his spine, hardening his cock. He closed his eyes, dropped his head back and let her possess him. For a moment he let the dark images fade, fought to find his humanity, what was left of it.

What she hadn't taken from him.

If he was more honest, some of it he had given

away. There, on the bed, in the moonlight, with her hand stirring his blood, it would be easy to tell himself he hadn't had a choice, but that would be a lie.

He lifted his head, took her hand and began kissing her knuckles. Gently, he worked his way down, skimming over each one. "Lie back," he said, releasing her hands.

She did as he asked, settling back onto the pillows, her face turned upward, her emerald eyes vibrant. "Stop screwing around and do it, Hayden."

He lifted her skirt, exposing her bare pussy, then watched her spread her legs. "It can be more than fucking."

"No. It can't."

Her words cut through the illusion in his mind, but he rejected them and the truth they held. "You mean you don't want it to be."

She sat up, grabbed his ass, and pulled his hips toward her. The tip of his cock bumped her wet opening. He braced himself, held his body stiff enough that she wasn't yet able to force him inside her. "You can get anyone to do this," he said. "You don't need me."

"But I want you, Hayden." She dug her fingers into his ass, pulled his butt cheeks apart. "I like the way you fuck me." Her fingernails cut into his skin as she squeezed harder. "You like it too."

The muscles in his legs started to shake. "We had a deal, the informa—"

"Is mine," she replied, grinding the words out between her teeth.

"We had a deal," he said again as he began losing the battle to keep his cock from her icy cunt. Using the

159

grip on his ass, she lowered his body, forced him in. "No. I don't like it. Don't want this." His cock was fully inside, being squeezed by her slick, cool pussy. "Or you, like this."

"What do you want Hayden?" She loosened her hold, let him pull away, but kept her grip firm. "What you had with your sweet girlfriend, Rachelle?"

"At least that was honest, consensual. No one was getting used."

She squeezed, pulling him down on top of her until their hips ground together. The sensation was too much to ignore, and he found himself moving against her. "I never took advantage of—"

"There you go again, being small minded." She spread her thighs, angled her ass upward.

"What about Matthew?" Hayden continued moving, now gliding in and out of her on his own, his resentment turning into that new dark energy. How long until that became permanent? Something he couldn't get rid of or control? Since when did he just give up, give in? He slowed, opened his eyes to look at Mattie. "He used you, didn't he? Used you the way he used Rachelle. And me."

Her words spilled out in a tense rush. "Stop talking about him."

He clamped his jaw shut and drove in, pistoning faster, letting himself feel each thrust. The past week ran through his mind, a blur of images and sensations. None good. "Did he hurt your feelings? Are you pissed because he doesn't want to use you anymore?"

She froze, her entire body stilled as she grabbed at him. He fought her, but this time wrapping one arm under her, trying to fuck her instead of resisting. She pried his arm out, then lifted him, breaking their contact. With one long sweep, she threw him into the air. His elbow smacked the wall, then be tumbled to the floor. She rolled onto her side, stretching as she used one hand to prop herself up. "You really have no idea what's going on Hayden. I tried to help you, get what I needed and keep you out of it, but you're *so fucking smart.*"

He shifted, leaned his back against the wall. "Help me?"

Outside, the wind howled and snow smacked on the windowpanes. Finally, after a long silence, she sighed. "At least you think you're smart."

His mind spun with possibilities. What wasn't he seeing? What had he missed?

She sat up, looked down at him. "Did you ever ask yourself why you got yourself in to this?"

That night in the library belonged to a different life. "Student loans," he replied. His resentment was misplaced, but he indulged himself and added, "Something you don't know anything about, I'm sure."

"That's it? You were stressed about your bills?"

He wasn't going to admit that he'd thought writing the best crap for Bob's rag of a paper would somehow land him a job at *The Globe*. Sitting there on the floor, naked, with his dick sticking out, that seemed like the most asinine of possibilities.

She leaned downward, her hair blocking the light from the street. Smirking, she waved toward his still hard cock. "Thought you didn't want me?"

That had been a lie. But so what? She'd lied too, and he wanted to turn that back at her. "What have you done to help me? Not one single thing."

161

She lay back down, spread her thighs, put her hands between her legs and started stroking her clit. The motion was so like Matthew. He watched her fingers. "What the fuck is wrong with you?"

The green from her eyes glimmered from the bed. "I need it."

"I'm not going to fuck you. I'm done with that. I'm done with all this."

She stared at him but didn't respond as she continued stoking herself, her fingers slipping in-between her slick folds. The blood in his veins started to thrum, pulsing downward to his cock.

"You can give it to me. Or I can come take it from you. Your choice."

He moved toward her, breathing in the raw, icy scent, felt that metallic sheen coat his throat. Salvia trickled downward, sending a chill down his neck. "One last time." He put his knee on the bed and thought about the ice-packed bodies on the other side of the wall. "But not again after this."

She lifted her hand and tucked it, along with the other, behind her head. "That's what they all say," she said, then closed her eyes.

His other knee was on the bed now, he was crawling forward. "I'm different."

"Prove it." Looking at him with one eye, she said, "Fuck me one last time, then see if you can walk away." She closed the eye. "See if I'll let you."

Knees between her thighs, he spread himself across her, then reached down and guided his cock in. After he slid his arms under her pale neck, he lowered his head and swallowed into the bitterness in his mouth. He'd become so accustomed to her body, that fucking her took no concentration. His hips moved automatically, and he was glad so little effort or concentration was required. Emotion? There was none of that either. None except the blackness that seeped in to his mind, blocking out what should've been there--something that would have meant the mindless coupling was what he wanted, something that mattered.

"Slow down," she said, turning her face and trying to cover his mouth with her cool lips.

He moved his face away and continued pumping in to her.

"Wait." She tried again to kiss him, the second time she even added some tenderness as she whispered into his ear. "What if it could be different?"

It was only then that he realized she'd stopped moving with him. Her body was stiff, tense and cold. But it was too late to say anything, or do anything different. He was already coming, the frantic, hard spasms squeezing the cum from his cock, spilling it inside her.

"Did you come?" he asked.

No reply, no movement. A long minute passed until the soft rustle of the bed cover cut through the silence. "You couldn't tell?"

No, not that time.

She'd moved to sit beside him. He was looking for a green gleam, thought he saw something, but it could have been light from the street. "Do you care?"

"No." That was the truth. "Like I said, last time."

Rough laughter came from her throat as she continued writhing on the bed, bending and curling with an uncanny combination of beauty and evil. So wrong. Everything about her.

"I don't care what you do to me. I'm not living like this." He gestured to her. "Like that."

More mocking laughter from the thing he'd let ruin his life. Somewhere inside himself he searched for the last shreds of his ragged dignity. This was the end, whatever it was going to be he'd take it. He didn't want the notes. Or the journal. Or one more minute of this disgusting shitstorm. "Go look in my bathroom."

That made her stop, every muscle in her body locked into place. One of her eyebrows twisted. She mouth pulled into that all-knowing smirk.

He watched the curl of her mouth and then stared into her eyes. Nothing in her expression changed.

All in.

He tensed, knowing that his command to her changed everything. Jerking his chin toward the door, he said. "Go. Do it."

She got up, stood up in front of him, intentionally showing off her powerful body for a few seconds before turning around and stalking away. The quick thud of her bare feet on the wood floor faded, then stopped. Then nothing but the thump of his heart. Those bodies were the only bargaining chip he had. Giving them up should send her back to Matthew, get her back into his good graces, so she could go back to doing whatever nefarious shit she wanted.

Moments later, the apartment was still quiet. He got up, went through the dark hall, then eased open the bathroom door. She sat on edge of the tub, her mass of hair hanging down, blocking her face from his view. She'd pulled the burlap from the thing's face and was stroking its cheek. The body had shoulder length brown hair, delicate eyebrows but a strong, bold nose.

Its mouth was closed, lips chapped and chalky white. Its skin was the same, chalky, but with an olive tone. Man or woman, it was impossible to tell.

"He must be pissed about this." She tucked some of the strands of hair behind its ear then without waiting for a response, she pulled the burlap from the other's face. The second one was clearly female, but how old he was, he couldn't' tell. Maybe in her early 20s. Mattie ran a fingertip under the girl's chin, then turned to where Hayden was standing in the doorway. "Going to tell me how you managed to get these from Guy?"

By the time his surprise passed over his face he knew it was too late to brother hiding it. "How did you know it was Guy who had them?"

"I'm the one who delivered them." She folded her arms under her massive tits and watched his face. "Don't tell me you thought that asshole somehow managed to sneak into the camp and steal dormants during my watch?"

He grabbed a towel from the rack, wrapped it around his waist, then moved to the window. Flecks of white swirling in the streetlights, then moving off into the night. It was constant, this storm, her insidiousness. He nudged the window open, letting the chill in. The bitter air moved across him, so much like her, always there and trying to get inside his skin. "I guess I didn't know it was your watch."

Her mouth pulled tight as she slid him a look. "Why do you think Matthew was in my face about it?"

Not that he cared anymore, but she had a point.

She turned away from him, back to the bodies in his tub. "Thanks for helping me out, Hayden. Again."

165

Using both hands, she covered the girl's face then pulled the burlap over the other's, covering everything but its chin. She spoke softly. "I'm taking them back, you know."

"If you didn't want Guy to have them, why did you give him them in the first place?"

She tossed one of the ice bags onto the floor. "Tit for tat. Isn't that always the way?"

Right. He was Plan B. Getting what she wanted on her own, plan A. "Did you get what you wanted from Guy?" Fuck. She'd used him so thoroughly, sucked him in so completely. And he'd let her.

"You already know the answer to that. And thanks to you, it didn't cost me anything." More half-melted bags of ice hit the floor as she continued flinging the bags. "In fact, now I'll look like a hero, bringing these back." A bag hit the floor with a hard thump, then slid onto Hayden's foot. Icy water slid down between his toes.

He kicked the bag toward the tub. It left a wet trail across the tiles. "I'm done with all this fucked up shit."

"What about your article? What about your loans?" The last bag flew through the air, hit the pile with a soft rustle. Her hands were dripping with cold water. She leaned her back against the wall and cupped her breasts, pinched her nipples, making them peaked and wet. "What about your sweet girlfriend Rachelle?"

Dragging his gaze from her tits, he snarled, "Fuck you."

"Yeah, fuck you too, Hayden." Her breasts, still slick and tight, bounced when she let go of them, then swung as she stood. "Now that I got what I wanted

166

from Guy, I don't need you anymore," she said, then brushed past him into the hall.

Tugging the towel tighter around his hips, he followed her to his bedroom, watched her snatch up her things from his bed. Silently, she slipped into her skirt, then bound her breasts with the red straps. After her tightening her boots, she grabbed her leather and slid it over her shoulders as she headed back to the bathroom. He followed, found her lifting the first of the two bodies up onto her shoulder. He knew from his own experience with them that they were lighter than they looked, so he wasn't surprised to see her heft the second up onto the other shoulder. He stepped back, watched her strut down his hall, stopping at the door. He slipped around her, yanked the door open. Without even a sideways glance, she worked herself through the threshold, out onto the landing, then started down the steps.

No last word. Not even a last nasty look.

She was just gone.

With a light shove, he closed the door.

Chapter Twelve
"Tit for tat. Isn't that always the way?"

About 12 hours later, after a shockingly successful day at work, Hayden approached his building. The piece he'd done on the convention had generated way more hits than it was worth. The pictures he'd taken of Guy sure had come in handy. The ones he'd used for the piece—and the ones he'd used to convince the man to whip up some sketches in a hurry—were pure genius. The sketches Hayden had sent in to accompany the photo of Guy claimed to be from the zombie tracker's most recent experiences with the tribe. The scene of human sex slaves tied to trees looked a hell of a lot like the ones from the book, but the readers didn't give a shit. They just wanted to believe that kind of horror had been going on just miles from the city. What if they knew the truth? Had lived through it like he had?

A nasty gust whipped across Hayden's face, grabbing his scarf, making it fly out in front of him. He tucked it back into his coat, and started toward his place, thinking about whether he'd be celebrating with a beer or if he'd finally open that bottle of Luis Felipe his uncle had given him for graduation.

It wasn't the celebration he'd wanted, those connections he'd been trying to pry from Bob would have to come later. Hayden didn't give a shit. He'd gotten the pieces done. Bob was more than satisfied. Mattie was gone. Rachelle was talking to him again, promising to be around later with another surprise. Every time he wondered how she'd come out of that experience unscathed, he pushed the questions and fears to the back of his mind. Just be glad it's over. Just be glad she's not asking questions. No questions meant no answers and no answers meant not telling the truth. Those were all lies and secrets he'd be taking to the grave.

The fresh piles of snow blocked the corner and he had to slow to climb through them. Hunks of ice slipped into his pants and sent shivers up his calves. He didn't care. In minutes, he'd be kicking his boots off, peeling off his socks, shaking his pants down and getting naked. Should he invite himself over to Rachelle's or invite her to his? His had a bigger bed, hotter water. He slid his phone out, ready to tell her to meet him there when he spotted her coming down the apartment steps. She was wearing the fur and carrying a cardboard box. She moved slowly, her gaze focused on the ice-covered steps.

He hurried to meet her at the bottom. "Hey," he said when she nearly slammed into him.

She stopped short, the box shook as she looked up, her face blank. "Hey."

The sleeve of her favorite sweater hung down the side of the box. An old pair of sweatpants, a pile of books and her favorite coffee mug—the one she always drank out of first thing in the morning when she spent the night—were crowded together.

Hayden opened his mouth to apologize, again, for

what he didn't even know but it seemed the only way to get her to stop, but a familiar voice stopped him short.

"Yo, Hayden."

Matthew brushed past him, shoving his bony shoulder into him.

Rachelle's gaze darted from the box to Hayden to Matthew then back to Hayden. "I'm— I—"

"Rachelle? What are you doing?"

"It's obvious, isn't it, Hayden?" Matthew said, standing beside Rachelle.

"Fuck you," Hayden replied. As soon as the words were out of his mouth, he took a step back, out of Matthew's quick reach. Rachelle shrugged. "Semester's over, I can just hang out for a while."

He stared at the coffee mug. "Why?"

Her hair caught in the wind, and she reached up to brush it from her face. "I want to."

Hayden's stomach tensed and then rolled. "You're going back to the camp?"

"Yeah." She shifted the box so it sat on her hip, creating a barrier between them. "They like me. And its fun."

Matthew put his hand on Rachelle's back, guiding her down the steps.

When Rachelle reached the sidewalk, she handed the box to Matthew, then came back up the steps. "I know about the tea, Hayden. Mattie told me. She told me everything."

"Rachelle, you don't remember what happened there." He set his hand on her waist. "You need—"

She blinked and moved away from him, back toward Matthew. "Fuck off, Hayden."

He followed her down the steps. "They didn't tell you everything. You don't understand what hap—"

"You're the one who doesn't understand." Matthew had met Rachelle halfway, his long fingers pale against the brown box as he took it. "For one thing, you don't understand my sister at all. Not one bit. You're the one she didn't tell everything."

Matthew smirked and walked away, heading back to the battered green Chevy truck parked between a black Audi A4 and Mercedes wagon. Rachelle turned and jogged after him. Matthew, put the box in the back, dug around in the bed, then came back with a coil of rope and a thermos. Rachelle drank what was offered to her, then lifted her hands, putting her wrists together. She climbed into the truck cab, scooted over to the passenger side then stared straight ahead.

Hayden turned. The doorway of the brownstone was empty, the steps clear. Even though it was dark outside, it wasn't that late, so most of the windows of the building were yellow with light. There was nothing unusual there, except a long narrow shadow on the roof. It wasn't a shadow, Hayden realized. It was *her*, lying across the steep roof, her long net-covered legs stretched out behind her, her entire body still, stiff and cold, her eyes growing green.

About the Author

Isabelle Drake got her start writing confession stories for pulp magazines like *True Confessions* and *True Love*. Since publishing those first few stories she has written in multiple genres, earned an MFA in Creative Writing and became an English & Writing Professor.

When away from her keyboard, she watches films, especially classic noir, horror and romance, and reads (of course). An avid traveler, she'll go just about anywhere--at least once--to meet people and get ideas.

Find Isabelle as Isabelle Drake on Facebook, Youtube and Goodreads & @isabelledrake on Instagram, Twitter and Tumblr & isadrake on Snapchat.

If You Like This Title, You Might Also Like

Gone with the Dead: An Anthology of Romance and Horror
Edited by Lori Perkins

Still Hungry for Your Love
Edited by Lori Perkins

A Tribute Anthology to Deadworld Creator Gary Reed
Edited by Lori Perkins

An Outcast State
By Scott D. Smith

Evoluzion: Smarter Zombies, Smarter Weapons, Vol. 1
By James V. Smith, Jr.

Redemzion, Vol. 2 in the Evoluzion Military Zombie series
By Axl Abbott

Stepford SoldierZ
By Axl Abbott

Demon with a Comb-Over
By Stuart R. West

Capricorn" Cursed
Book One of the Witch Upon a Star Series
By Sephera Giron

Aquarius: Haunted Heart
Book Two of the Witch Upon a Star Series
By Sephera Giron

Pisces: Teacher's Pet
Book Three of the Witch Upon a Star Series
By Sephera Giron

Aries: Swinging into Spring
Book Four of the Witch Upon a Star Series
By Sephera Giron

Made in the USA
Middletown, DE
12 August 2022